"I'll drive you home, Octavia."

She knew there was nothing she would have liked better. All the same, she said instantly in a tart voice, "You've made me jump! Thank you for the offer, but I've already made arrangements."

"Cancel them."

She turned to look at him. "And supposing I don't want to?" she inquired with deceptive mildness.

His mildness more than equaled hers. "I hope you will change your mind. I would like to talk to you."

"What about?" She had turned away from him and was giving an answering wave to a passenger going ashore.

"Will you marry me, Octavia?"

She whipped round to stare at him blankly…

Romance readers around the world were sad to note the passing of **Betty Neels** in June 2001. Her career spanned thirty years, and she continued to write into her ninetieth year. To her millions of fans, Betty epitomized the romance writer, and yet she began writing almost by accident. She had retired from nursing, but her inquiring mind still sought stimulation. Her new career was born when she heard a lady in her local library bemoaning the lack of good romance novels. Betty's first book, *Sister Peters in Amsterdam,* was published in 1969, and she eventually completed 134 books. Her novels offer a reassuring warmth that was very much a part of her own personality, and her spirit and genuine talent will live on in all her stories.

THE BEST *of*

BETTY NEELS

Never While the Grass Grows

TORONTO NEW YORK LONDON
AMSTERDAM PARIS SYDNEY HAMBURG
STOCKHOLM ATHENS TOKYO MILAN MADRID
PRAGUE WARSAW BUDAPEST AUCKLAND

ISBN-13: 978-0-373-19986-0

NEVER WHILE THE GRASS GROWS

This edition published by arrangement with Harlequin Books S.A.

For questions and comments about the quality of this book please contact us at Customer_eCare@Harlequin.ca.

www.Harlequin.com

Printed in U.S.A.

CHAPTER ONE

SISTER OCTAVIA LOCK swept through the swing doors of Casualty on a wave of vague ill-humour; she had over-slept and as a consequence had had no breakfast save a cup of tea, drunk far too hot and as much toast as she could cram into her mouth with one bite, and over and above that, it was a glorious September morning with enough of autumn in the air to make her wish that she was at home and not in a London hospital, hemmed in by narrow streets and rows of shabby little houses. And now, to make matters worse, she could see at a glance that Casualty, even at eight o'clock in the morning, was already filling itself up fast. Her senior, Sister Moody, who tended to take her time in coming on duty after breakfast, would as a consequence doubtless live up to her name. Octavia's eye lighted upon a small forlorn boy sitting by himself and, her ill-humour forgotten, she swept him along with her on the way to the office, asking his name and what was the matter as they went. 'Stanley,' he told her tearfully, and his mum had sent him along because he'd burnt his arm the day before.

Octavia sighed, popped him into a cubicle and began to take off his too-small jacket. It amazed her that although patients crowded into Casualty, a vast number of them took their time about it. And if I'd been this mum I'd have brought Stanley here pretty smartly, she reflected, gently laying bare a sizeable burn wrapped in a handkerchief. The blisters weren't broken, and that was something to be thankful for; she slid the handkerchief away and replaced it with gauze, said: 'OK Stanley, the doctor will come and make that much more comfortable for you,' warned a student nurse about him, and went into the office. One of the night Sisters was already there ready to leave and Octavia listened carefully to the night report, happily short and fairly uneventful, before she remarked gloomily: 'You may have had a good night, Joan, but I've a nasty feeling that we're in for a perfectly foul day—are you on tonight?'

Her companion grinned smugly. 'Nights off—you'll have Snoopy Kate on…'

'Oh, lord, and I'm on till nine o'clock. Sister Moody wants the evening; I'll have to have a split.' She paused and smiled suddenly: 'It's my weekend off, though.'

They parted then, Joan to breakfast and bed, Octavia into Casualty to cast an eye over the patients already being treated and then those who were waiting. There was nothing urgent; cuts and bruises, septic fingers, a fractured collarbone which a nurse had already put into a collar and cuff, a number of small children with earache, sore throats and the like and the usual sprinkling of elderly men and women for morning dressings and stitches to be removed. She had just finished her round when Sister Moody arrived, nodded briefly and retired to the office, to stay there for a good deal of the day, doing the paper work and only coming out when an urgent case came in; not that she did much to help then; explaining comfortably to Octavia that at her age it would be ridiculous to expect her to take too active a part in the work while Octavia was perfectly capable of coping.

Octavia started her daily round of the cubicles and dressing rooms and small theatre, checking this and that with care but not wasting time. Nurses would be going to their coffee break in an hour and the quicker the light cases were dealt with the better. She could hear the steady hum of voices through the theatre door and all the sounds that went with it; the clatter of bowls, the faint click of instruments tossed into receivers, the telephone—she would have to go and give a hand. All the same, she paused by a window and gazed out into the street outside, full of traffic and people hurrying to work, a tall girl with a splendid figure and a lovely face crowned by rich brown hair, drawn back neatly under her cap, although a number of small curls had escaped to frame her face. Her eyes were hazel, large and heavily fringed and topped by black brows and her mouth curved gently, and as though these weren't enough, she had a happy nature, marred only occasionally by a fiery temper. She turned away from the window presently and went back into Casualty, rolling up her sleeves as she went.

The day went as most days went; a steady trickle of minor casualties, interrupted frequently by the more severely injured as well as a small girl with a perforated appendix and an elderly man who had been found alone, half starved and dirty in a pokey little room in one of the rows of small houses close to the hospital. He had opened weary eyes as Octavia bent over him and told her fretfully to leave him alone, 'Because what's the use of getting me on my feet again?' he wanted to know. 'I've nowhere to go and no one to bother about me.'

Octavia, taking his blood pressure, gave him a motherly smile. 'You just wait,' she admonished him kindly, 'there's no reason why you shouldn't be fit enough to get a job. You just need fattening up, you know. How old are you?'

'Sixty—who'd want the likes of me, I'd like to know?'

'Let's worry about that when the time comes—first we'll get you better.' She turned at the tap on her shoulder. 'Here's the doctor to have a look at you.'

He had pneumonia, not badly—nothing that a few days in hospital wouldn't put right. Octavia arranged for him to be admitted to the men's medical ward and when he asked her if she would visit him, promised cheerfully that she would.

'Now that's a great shame,' she declared to John Waring, the Casualty Officer. 'A nice man like that thrown out of work because the family went to Switzerland—the least they could have done would have been to try and get him fixed up with someone else, or even taken him with them—I mean, after fifteen years working for them,' she paused. 'I'm not sure what a handyman does…'

'Makes himself handy,' and then more seriously: 'I agree with you, Octavia, and he hasn't much chance of getting any work—I suppose he would be unskilled labour, and he's getting on.' John finished the notes he was writing up and looked up at her. 'Are you off this evening? How about a film?'

She shook her head regretfully. 'I'm off…' she glanced at the clock, 'now, then I'm on until nine and I'll be fit for nothing by then.'

'Tomorrow, then?'

'Lovely—but aren't you on call?'

He grinned at her. 'I'll get someone to stand in for me.'

A nice boy, she reflected as she went through the hospital on her way to lunch and off duty. She had been out with him several times, indeed she had been out with most of the housemen in St Maud's at one time or another, for she was popular with everyone and as pretty as a picture to boot, but although a surprisingly large percentage of them had wanted to marry her, she had remained heartwhole.

By the time she had reached the canteen and joined her friends at table, she had forgotten all about John Waring.

She returned to Casualty just before six o'clock, to find it almost as full as when she had left it and Sister Moody waiting impatiently for her.

'There's a query appendix in the end bay,' she was told swiftly, 'a scalp wound next to it, and then a Colles fracture…' she was ticking the cases off on her fingers, 'a crushed thumb, septic foot…the rest haven't been seen yet. Nurse Barnes is taking their names now—John Waring will be down presently. We had a couple of RTAs in—they're warded—oh, and a BID I've had no time to make up the book.' She was already half way through the door as she spoke and now, with a briefly muttered goodnight, she was gone.

There were two student nurses on duty as well as Mrs Taylor, a reliable nursing aide who had been in Casualty for so long that no one could remember when she had first come; she was elderly now and not able to lift or do any heavy work, but she was invaluable because she knew where everything was and fetched it at the drop of a hat. Octavia sent her to help the senior of the student nurses to marshall the remainder of the patients ready for John Waring and took the other nurse with her to deal with the appendix first and then, seeing that the man was resting comfortably, to get the scalp wound cleaned up, something Sister Moody might have done and hadn't.

It was almost nine o'clock, after a steady stream of patients had been dealt with, that the street entrance was flung open and a tall man with wide shoulders and a giant's stride came in. He was carrying a little old lady in his arms and rather to Octavia's surprise, walked across the department to deposit her carefully on a couch in one of the bays. Only then did he turn to address her.

'Mugged,' his voice was deep and unhurried. 'You're in charge? Well, get the Casualty Officer here at once, will you?'

Octavia, bending over the small figure, paused for a moment to look up at the man. She said evenly: 'Thanks for bringing her in, you can safely leave the rest to us now.'

He was a handsome man, with fair hair liberally sprinkled with grey, looking down his high-bridged nose with cold blue eyes. He looked, she realised suddenly, as though he didn't like her. With something of an effort she clung to her professional calm and then found it in shreds when he went on: 'I shall remain until she has received adequate treatment.'

Octavia let out an indignant snort and managed to hold her tongue. She could deal with the tiresome man presently, but now she bent to her patient, taking off the battered felt hat to search for head wounds, taking her pulse moving her arms gently and when the old lady opened her eyes, asked quietly: 'Can you tell me where it hurts, my dear? You're quite safe now, in hospital, but I don't want to move you too much until we know what the damage is.'

The old eyes studied her wearily. 'I aches all over, but there ain't much sense in bothering over me, I 'aven't got a soul ter mind if I snuffs it.'

'I for one shall mind,' Octavia assured her warmly. She ignored the large man looming over her and told the student nurse hovering to telephone Doctor Waring.

'Tell him it's a mugging, an elderly lady, no visible fractures, contusion on temple, cut eye, cut lip, not yet fully examined, rather shocked. Ask him to come at once, please.'

She began very gently to take off the old lady's coat, a shockingly shabby garment, now freshly torn and ruined for ever. Octavia got out her scissors. 'Look, my dear, I'm going to cut your coat so that I can get it off without hurting you; we'll replace it for you.'

She had been busy cutting up one sleeve, and now when she went to do the same with the other, the patient's rescuer took the scissors from her. It was then that she saw that his knuckles were bleeding and that there was a small cut across the back of one hand, the blood congealing now.

'Oh, you're hurt!' She added forcefully: 'I hope you knocked them down and jumped on them!'

Her companion continued his steady plying of the scissors. 'I knocked them down—they—er—hardly needed to be jumped on, I fancy.'

She was easing the old lady's jumper and put out her hand for the scissors again. 'Good for you,' said Octavia, 'now if you wouldn't mind just going into the next cubicle, Nurse will clean that hand up and the doctor can take a look at it. You'll need ATS too—a knife, I imagine?'

'You imagine correctly, Sister.'

She nodded without looking at him. 'I'm going to telephone the police very shortly, perhaps you wouldn't mind telling them just what happened? This little lady is hardly fit to be questioned just yet. We shall need your name and address too... Nurse will see to it.' She turned as she heard John Waring's step. 'Hullo, again.' She flashed him a tired smile. 'I've not done too much—I thought you'd better take a quick look first. There's a small wound here...' They bent over the patient together, everything else forgotten for the moment.

It was some time later, when Octavia had discovered her patient's name, wrapped her in a dressing gown, Mr Waring had dealt with her injuries, and she had taken her to X-ray and finally seen her safely off to one of the women's wards, that she discovered that the man who had brought her in was still there. The police had come and gone, John

Waring had disappeared too and she had sent the two nurses and Mrs Taylor off duty. It was ten o'clock by now and she had started to tidy up the cubicle before writing up the Casualty Book. Snoopy Kate hadn't been near—typical, thought Octavia, racing round the little room transforming it to its usual spick and span appearance; when there was nothing to do, she would bustle around, picking holes in things that didn't matter at all, but when the day staff were delayed by a case, Snoopy Kate kept well away until everything was quiet again. Octavia shot the last receiver into its allotted space and nipped across to the office to be brought to a halt by a voice behind her.

'This place is very inefficiently run,' remarked the big man coolly. 'You send your nurses off duty and remain behind to do work which is theirs; and apparently there is no one to take over—just when do you go yourself?'

Octavia, quite short-tempered by now, answered him snappily: 'I might ask the same question of you. Doctor Waring saw you, didn't he? and Nurse told me that your hand had been attended to. And really it is no concern of yours as to when I go off duty.' She was about to wish him goodnight and show him the door when she was struck by a sudden thought. 'Did you have your ATS?'

'Ah—I wondered when someone would give it a thought,' he told her nastily.

She whisked back to the trolley she had just tidied so carefully and found syringe, needle and ampoule. 'I'm sorry,' she told him contritely, 'you should have said sooner, but I quite see that you wouldn't want to do that because we were a bit busy. I hope it hasn't spoilt your evening...'

The man's lip quivered slightly. 'My evening was spoilt some hours ago,' he reminded her.

He had got to his feet and taken off his jacket and rolled

up a sleeve. Silk shirt, she noted, and a beautifully tailored jacket; she wondered fleetingly who he was. Rather an arrogant type, she considered, and given to saying just what he thought, but he had a nice voice and the trace of an accent…

'Why did you look like that when your patient told you that she had not a soul to mind?'

She stood beside him, the syringe in hand, her lovely eyes wide. 'Look like what?'

'Worried—upset, angry.'

She shot the needle into the arm like a tree trunk before she answered him. 'Oh, well—there was a man this morning, the police brought him in, half starved and ill and elderly—he said almost the same thing.' She added almost to herself: 'There must be someone…'

'You like helping lame dogs?' He had his jacket on again.

She said indignantly: 'That sounds horrid, as though I were a do-gooder, but everyone deserves a chance to be happy and have enough to eat and a home.'

He sat down again and she interrupted herself to ask: 'Don't you want to go? There's nothing more…'

He glanced at his watch. 'I'll stay until you go off duty—anyone might come in and you're alone.'

He was nice after all. Octavia gave him a friendly smile. 'That's very nice of you—do you imagine that the muggers will come crawling in here to have their bruises seen to? I'm not easily frightened—besides, one of the night Sisters will be here any time now.'

'Ah, yes,' he murmured, 'Snoopy Kate. Nurse told me about her while she was cleaning up my hand—she sounds interesting. I believe I hear footsteps now.'

It was Snoopy Kate right enough, coming in from the other end of Casualty so that she could peer and prod at the equipment and move all the trollies half an inch, tut-tutting as she came. She could see Octavia but no one else and she began grumbling while she was still the length of the department away. 'Ten o'clock,' she declared, 'and still not finished. I don't know, you girls can't work like we did when I was young— What are you doing here anyway? There's no patient…'

The large man came into view then, holding his strapped knuckles rather ostentatiously before him, so that Octavia, suppressing a grin was able to point out to her superior that there was indeed a patient. 'This gentleman brought in an old lady who had been injured by muggers,' she told her, and added coldly: 'A few minutes before nine o'clock, but since I wasn't relieved and there was a lot to do, I'm only just finished.'

Snoopy Kate shot a look at the man, who was looking down his nose again, looking detached and a little bored. 'I was hindered,' she explained awkwardly. 'I'll take over now, Sister.'

'No need,' Octavia told her cheerfully. 'He's ready to go and I've finished the clearing up. The book'll take me two minutes.' She nodded a general goodnight and went into the office and shut the door. She could hear Snoopy Kate questioning the man while she made her entries and smiled to herself. He was quite nice, she conceded, but he had been rude to begin with and obviously liked his own way and wasn't above being sarcastic, although Nurse Scott should have remembered the ATS—she would have to speak to her in the morning. She heard a door creak and the rustle of Snoopy Kate's uniform. They had gone. She closed the book, and went back into Casualty on her way to her bed at last. The man was still there.

'Oh, I'm going,' he told her blandly. 'That was a nasty

trick, leaving me to parry your colleague's questions—you seem to have a grudge against me.'

He was smiling and he looked nicer than ever. 'It was mean of me,' she allowed, 'but you were rather nasty when you came in this evening, you know. Just as though you expected everyone to do exactly what you said at once—I see in the book that you're a professor, so I expect that accounts for it. Teaching people must make you a bit bossy—boys or girls?' she asked.

The face he turned to hers was without expression. 'Both.' He went to the door. 'I hope—no, I *know* that we shall meet again, Sister. Goodnight.'

Octavia was halfway to the Nurses' Home when she remembered that she had promised to visit the man who had been admitted that morning. It was late; most patients would have been settled for the night, but she could just take a peep. She whispered to the staff nurse in charge of Men's Medical and went quietly down the ward to find him awake. He looked quite different now; he had been shaved and bathed and put into clean pyjamas and looked ten years younger, although woefully thin. He smiled when he saw her.

'I said ter meself: She'll come, and yer 'ave. Looked after me a treat, they 'ave, too.'

'Splendid. Now, Mr…'

'Call me Charlie, Sister.' He looked wistful. 'Like friends…'

She took a hand, still ingrained with grime despite the washing, and held it firmly in hers. 'Friends it is,' she told him, 'and now you just listen to me, Charlie, you just lie there and eat and sleep for a day or two and don't worry about a thing. I feel in my bones that your luck's changed. And now go to sleep, there's a dear.' Upon which heartening words she bade him goodnight.

She went to see him each day after that, watching his face slowly fill out and his eyes brighten. The Ward Sister was a friend of hers, so it didn't take much persuasion to get her to recommend that Charlie should stay where he was for another week at least. And she went to see the little old lady, Mrs Stubbs, too, smaller than ever in a hospital nightgown and with her grey hair neatly arranged over her bruised head. She had a black eye too, which gave her a decidedly rakish air, but despite her injuries she insisted on sitting out of bed each day and before very long had coaxed the nurses to let her do any little odd jobs of mending or sewing. She was, the Ward Sister told Octavia, very good with her needle.

'Well, surely a job could be found for her?' asked Octavia. 'What about the sewing room?'

'Huh—two were made redundant last month. The Social Worker's scouting round though and there's at least a week before discharge—longer, I imagine.'

The week neared its end and Octavia, weary from the rush and urgency of a constantly busy Casualty, went happily off duty on the Friday evening. She had been to see Charlie and Mrs Stubbs and it seemed reasonable to suppose that they would still be there when she returned on Monday afternoon. They were making progress now, but as yet their futures were uncertain; a problem which somehow had come to be very important to her. She caught the train by the skin of her teeth and found it crowded and resigned herself to standing in the corridor until Guildford, where she got a seat, crushed between a stout elderly lady and a small boy who ate crisps for the rest of the journey. She was kept so busy brushing crumbs off her new skirt that she had no time or inclination to think of anything much and at Alresford she discovered that her father wasn't waiting for her, something which happened from time to time, for he was a Professor of Physics and remarkably absent-minded. She could telephone from the station, but on the other hand it would be as quick—quicker, to take a taxi.

Her home was in the centre of the little town, a small Georgian town house in a row of similar dwellings. It had no garden in the front, but tucked away at the back was a pleasant walled lawn with flower beds and vegetables, kept alive by Octavia's care on her frequent but brief visits. She opened the front door now and went into the narrow hall just as Mrs Lovelace, the daily housekeeper, came from the kitchen, dressed to leave.

'There you are, Miss Octavia,' she remarked comfortably. 'There's supper for you keeping hot, your pa's had his.' She nodded her head in its severe felt hat in the direction of one of the doors. 'Busy with something or other, he is—did he know you were coming? I did remind him, but he didn't hear, I imagine.'

Octavia smiled. 'He never does, Mrs Lovelace. Thanks for the supper.' She put down her case and took off her gloves. 'I'm starved!'

'And I've no doubt of that,' declared the housekeeper. 'I doubt you get good wholesome food in those hospitals. Can you manage if I don't come in tomorrow?'

'Yes, of course—I'll have to go back on Sunday evening, though. I'll get Father's supper before I go.'

Mrs Lovelace nodded. 'Thank you, Miss Octavia. I'll be here Monday as usual.'

Professor Lock greeted his daughter with an absent-minded warmth which she took in good part; her father had always been absentminded, and now that he was elderly, he was worse than ever. She kissed his bald pate, begged him not to disturb himself—something she was well aware he had no intention of doing, anyway—and went along to the kitchen to see what was for her supper.

It smelled delicious; she took her case upstairs to the comfortable bedroom she had had since she was a child, and without bothering to unpack it, went downstairs again to put Mrs Lovelace's tasty steak and kidney pie on a tray and carry it along to her father's study. She ate in silence until he had finished what he was writing and then listened with interest to the theories he had been expounding. She wasn't in the least scientific herself, but she was intelligent enough to make sensible observations and was rewarded presently by his: 'You haven't my brain, my dear, but for a girl you don't do so badly.' He peered at her over his old-fashioned spectacles. 'Are you here for a weekend?'

She nodded, her mouth full of pie.

'You have been busy?'

'Well, yes—people have accidents all the time, you know, Father.'

'Indeed yes—I read only recently a most interesting article… Do you not wish to marry, Octavia? How old are you?'

'Twenty-seven, Father.'

'Your mother had been married five years… You have had the opportunity, I imagine?'

'Oh, yes—several times. But I never seem to meet the right man.' She got to her feet. 'I'll go and make some coffee, shall I?'

'That would be nice. I should like you to be married, Octavia. I've never been very good with money, as you know, what little I have is getting used up rapidly.' He frowned. 'Books have become increasingly expensive… There won't be much left for you, my dear.'

She smiled at him fondly. 'Don't worry, Father dear; I've got a good job, and I earn enough to keep myself—just you go on buying all the books you want. Anyway, you get fees for your articles, don't you, and all that coaching you do.'

He brightened. 'Ah, yes—I'd forgotten. What a comfort you are, Octavia. Your mother would have been proud of you.'

While she made the coffee she thought rather wistfully of her mother who had died ten years ago or more; a pretty, still young woman who had known how to manage her husband without him realising it; it was only since her death that he had become so withdrawn. A pity I haven't got a brother thought Octavia. She and her father got on splendidly and were devoted to each other, but sometimes she reflected that he would have managed quite well without her. Her fault perhaps for working away from home, but she had a good job now, with a chance of stepping into Sister Moody's shoes when that lady retired; the thought was somehow depressing. While she drank her coffee she reviewed the various men who had wanted to marry her; none of them were exactly what she was looking for. She wasn't quite sure what that was, herself, but she supposed she would know when she met him. She sighed gently and went to the kitchen to wash the supper things and then to bid her father a quiet goodnight before going upstairs to bed.

It was over breakfast the next morning that Mr Lock wanted to know why she didn't change her job. 'I realise that you would have to remain in nursing, because you don't know what else to do, do you? But why not strike out, my dear? Go abroad, travel, see something of the world.'

She stared at him, a little surprised, 'Me? Father, where would I go? There are jobs enough in the Middle East, but I don't want to live there, and it's not all that easy to go to Australia or New Zealand now—work permits, and so on, you know. I'd love to travel, though.' She wrinkled her forehead in thought. 'I could get a job with some rich elderly type who wanted to travel, but I should be bored in no time. I think I'll stay where I am.'

Her parent passed his cup to be refilled. 'Until you marry,' he commented.

Her father's unexpected interest in her ruffled the serenity of her weekend just a little. She did the shopping in the little town without her usual interest and although she accepted an invitation to have coffee with a chance acquaintance, she had to make an effort to take an interest in the conversation. Perhaps, she reflected uneasily, she had been drifting along and getting into a rut and should make an effort to get out of it before she no longer wanted to. She pondered about it during Sunday too, sitting beside her father in church, looking attentively at the vicar while he preached his sermon and not hearing a word of it.

She went back to London in the early evening, leaving her father quite happily immersed in his books, although he paused in his reading long enough to wish her a good journey back and expressed the hope that she would be home again soon. He said that every time she went home and she smiled at him now and said that yes, she would be back again in two weeks provided Sister Moody didn't want to change her weekend.

She reached the hospital just as most of her friends were coming off duty and because she was still feeling a little unsettled, she went along to the Sisters' sitting room to share their after supper tea. It had been a busy weekend, Sister Moody told her gloomily, although that lady's idea of business and her own didn't quite agree. 'I shan't come on until one o'clock tomorrow,' declared Sister Moody. 'I could do with a morning in bed—you've an evening, haven't you? So there'll be two of us on until five o'clock, it usually quietens down by then.'

Octavia agreed pleasantly; she hadn't found that Casualty ever quietened down, but she didn't say so. Presently she went to sit with her own particular friends, to listen to the day's gossip and talk the inevitable shop. It was as they were drinking the last dregs of their tea that Connie Wills, the junior Sister on Men's Medical, remarked: 'That nice old Charlie—you remember, Octavia? He's going on Thursday.'

Octavia put down her cup. 'He can't be—he's not fit—where's he going?'

'Well, it all turned out rather well. I know he's not fit, but someone—some man or other has offered him a job, living in—caretaking and so on. It's just up Charlie's street, and he's promised that Charlie shall be looked after and not allowed to work until he's quite well. Marvellous, isn't it?'

'That's funny,' chimed in the Sister, on Women's Surgical. 'Remember that little lady you sent us the other evening—the one you've been visiting? Well, she's got somewhere to go to, too. She's not to be discharged yet, but when she is, she's been offered this job helping the housekeeper in some house or other. All very vague, but quite OK, so John Waring tells me.'

'That's wonderful!' Octavia forgot her own vague problems in the pleasure of knowing that the unfortunate pair were to have more cheerful futures, after all. 'Tell Charlie I'll come to say goodbye, will you? I'll never get away in the morning—Monday…' she wrinkled her pretty nose, 'but I'll pop up and see Mrs Stubbs in the evening.'

They all went to their rooms after that, stopping to chat as they went, reluctant to bring their brief leisure to an end until Sister Moody, passing Octavia and a handful of the younger sisters still chatting outside their rooms, remarked sourly: 'Don't forget it's Monday tomorrow.'

They exchanged speaking glances and when she was

safely in the bathroom with the taps running, Octavia observed: 'Do you suppose we'll be like her in twenty years' time?'

'Not if I can help it,' declared Connie. 'I votes we get married.'

'Chance is a fine thing,' said Octavia.

They all looked at her. 'You've no reason to complain, Octavia, there's always someone or other dangling after you. It's us plain ones who worry.'

They all laughed as they broke up, but in her room, sitting on the side of her bed, Octavia mulled over that remark and felt a vague disquiet again. She was lucky, she knew that, but only because she was pretty—she knew that too, without conceit—but there would come a time, she supposed, when no one would dangle after her any more. Perhaps, she decided, hopping into bed, she should take the very next chance that came her way.

CHAPTER TWO

CASUALTY remained busy for the next few days; over and above the steady stream of broken bones and heads, street accidents, small children with beads up their noses and down their ears, and elderly persons with aches and pains with which they hadn't liked to bother their doctors, there was a bad fire in a high rise block of flats close to the hospital, and as well as some of its badly injured inmates, there were a number of firemen to be treated for the effects of smoke. Sister Moody, beside herself at having to work really hard, with little or no chance of taking refuge in her office, became as cross as two sticks, and because of that vented her vexation on the nurses. Octavia kept a tight hold on her patience and temper and breathed a sigh of relief when her superior took herself off for her weekend. True, they were now short of her services, but since these had been both grudgingly and sparingly given in the first place, it really didn't matter. Peace and harmony reigned once more even though they were all run off their feet.

It was Sunday evening, as Octavia sat writing up the books, when the Sister on Men's Medical put her head round the door. 'Still here?' she wanted to know. 'Who's relieving you?'

'Gill Sedgewick.'

'Her?' said Rhona ungrammatically. 'Let's hope she

remembers. Ever since she got married and took to part-time, she seems to think she's conferring a favour coming at all.' She came right in and perched on the desk. 'I say, Octavia—remember Suzy Preston?'

Octavia ruled a neat line and without glancing up said calmly: 'Well, of course I do, seeing she was a friend of mine—still is. I heard from her the other day—somewhere in Yorkshire, where she lives—she's gathering a wardrobe together and up in the clouds over that new job.'

'Well, she's not now. I just happened to be in the office this evening and Miss Bellamy and Mr Yates were in her office with the door open and I couldn't help over-hearing—actually, I did have to strain my ears a bit—Suzy's got an appendix and can't join the ship, and he was trying to persuade Miss B. to let him have someone in her place.'

'He'll be lucky. Poor old Suzy.' Octavia closed the Casualty book with a flourish. 'Where is she?'

'At home. Of course Mr Yates will get his own way—he always does; I mean having a brother who's a director of the shipping company helps a lot, and they always have our nurses, don't they? It's only a week before sailing time, besides, they think it impresses the passengers if they have one of us. After all, St Maud's is one of the best teaching hospitals in the country.'

Octavia piled her books neatly and got up. 'Oh, well, good luck to him. I must telephone Suzy, though. What rotten luck; she was so thrilled about it, too.' She sighed and glanced at her watch. 'I'm famished. I hope Gill comes soon. I must just see if the nurses are OK.'

She was with them when her relief arrived, and ten minutes later she was speeding out of the department, intent on getting away before another patient arrived.

Over supper there was a good deal of discussion about Suzy. She had caused quite a sensation when she had resigned to take a post as ship's nurse, besides stirring up a good deal of envy in her colleagues' bosoms; now the whole thing had fallen through and there was a good deal of conjecture as to what would happen. Rhona, repeating the conversation she had overheard, declared that one of them would find themselves on board the SS *Socrates* before the next week was out. 'For depend upon it,' she pointed out, 'old Yates will get his way, he always does—you know how he cuts his way through red tape and official forms when he's a mind to do so.'

They all left the table presently and wandered upstairs to the Sisters' sitting room in the nurses' home, to drink their bedtime tea and gossip, and Octavia went off to telephone Suzy, primed with enough questions and messages to keep her going throughout the night. But few of the questions were uttered; Suzy was in hospital, said her mother, under observation. She had had to give up her new job and expected to have the offending appendix removed within the next twenty-four hours. She had high hopes of being given a chance to re-apply for the job when she was well again.

Octavia offered sympathy, sent the most suitable of the messages and went back to the sitting room, where she told her news and settled down to write to Suzy. Everyone had messages, so she scratched away busily for several minutes, begged a stamp from someone and went along to post her letter.

The postbox by the hospital entrance hadn't been emptied yet; she slid the envelope inside, passing the time of day with Henry the night porter, and started back through the hospital. She had reached the back of the entrance hall when the Consultants' room door was flung open as she drew level with it, and Mr Yates came out. She wished him a polite goodnight without slackening her pace and then was halted in her tracks by his: 'Sister Lock—the very person I wanted to see. Will you come in here a minute?'

He held the door open and she went past him with a wordless calm which showed nothing of her sudden panic of mind while she tried to think why he should wish to see her at such a strange hour. Had something gone wrong in Casualty? She cast her mind back through the day and tried to remember if anything really awful had happened. True, she had had words with the laundry, and she had told one of the porters off for wanting to go to his dinner in the middle of transporting a patient to the operating theatre—surely he hadn't gone on strike? Her unease grew when Mr Yates lifted the receiver and asked for Miss Bellamy; something must be hideously wrong, but when that lady entered the room there was nothing in her impassive features to offer the smallest clue. She felt a little better when they both sat down and invited her to do the same, but she was quite unprepared for Mr Yates's opening remark.

'We are wondering if you would agree to taking Sister Preston's place on board the SS *Socrates*, Sister Lock. Probably you know that she is to have an appendicectomy tomorrow and at such short notice the shipping company are quite at a loss. My brother has asked my help in the matter and naturally I have discussed the matter with Miss Bellamy.' He paused to glance at the lady, who returned the look with an imperturbable one of her own. 'You seem to be the most suitable person to fill the gap; you have had a good deal of experience in theatre and the wards, and your record in Casualty is excellent.' He glanced at Octavia and then at the ceiling. 'A fortnight, you understand, and very pleasant work, I believe. After that time they should be able to find a nurse to take over until such time as Sister Preston can return to her duties.'

Octavia felt a surge of excitement at her learned companion's proposition, but she didn't allow it to show. 'Would I have to take the fortnight as part of my annual leave, Miss Bellamy?'

'Certainly not, Sister. You are to take two weeks' unpaid leave, as of course you will be paid while you are on the ship, and if you are worrying about Casualty, Sister Phipps can take over for that time; it just so happens that there will be no Sisters for her to relieve then.'

Octavia still hesitated and Mr Yates said briskly: 'No need to think it over, Sister, it's all quite straightforward—besides, you will see something of the world.' He coughed. 'The Mediterranean is delightful at this time of the year, pleasantly warm, and so much of interest to see.'

Just as though he were offering me a cruising holiday, thought Octavia, and said aloud: 'Clothes?'

'Uniform will be provided. I understand that the nurses and ship's doctors get a certain amount of shore leave.' Mr Yates looked vague. 'I'm sure you will know what to take.'

She cast him an amused glance and suddenly, for no reason at all, felt lighthearted about the whole affair. After all, why not? Life hadn't been much fun lately, she never met anyone…oh yes, she had, though, the bad-tempered giant in Casualty; he had arrived with no warning and gone again before she could discover anything about him. Oh, well, ships that pass…her thoughts were arrested by Miss Bellamy's calm voice asking her if she wished to accept the offer.

She heard herself doing just that, a little surprised because she hadn't really been thinking about it at all. 'But I should like a day or two in which to get ready,' she stated. 'When do I go?'

Mr Yates's: 'The *Socrates* sails on Saturday and you are to report for duty on Friday, you will be told when and where,' rather took her breath.

'I will arrange for you to leave your duties here on Tuesday evening, Sister. That will give you two days in which to prepare yourself.' Miss Bellamy smiled very faintly and when Octavia said: 'Yes, Miss Bellamy,' in a suitably meek voice, dismissed her graciously.

Once on the other side of the door, Octavia took to her heels. No nurse, and certainly no Sister, ran in corridors or wards unless there was fire or haemorrhage, but for once she forgot rules. She nipped up staircases and down passages at a splendid speed until she reached the Sisters' sitting room once more. They were all still there; Octavia closed the door behind her with a flourish and cried: 'Guess what?'

Everyone turned to look at her as she went on: 'I'm to stand in for Suzy on the *Socrates*...'

There was an immediate outburst of surprised voices as she went to perch on the arm of a chair. 'It's true,' she assured them, 'as I was passing the Consultants' room...' she plunged into her story.

Sister Moody took the news sourly and so, for that matter, did John Waring. Octavia's conciliatory: 'But it's only for two weeks,' was useless in the face of his unexpected annoyance, almost as though he had made up his mind that she was going away to spite him. She felt bewildered by it, because they had been good friends but never anything more, and her lack of conceit didn't allow of her realising that he was considered something of a celebrity in the doctors' quarters because he had been dating the beautiful Sister Lock for quite some time. She told him briskly not to behave like a crusty old man and was glad for once when their snatched conversation was brought to a close by the ambulance siren.

She had spent a wakeful hour or two during the night laying her plans; she would have to do some shopping;

Mr Yates had been right when he had said that she would know what to take—well, of course she would; any girl would, but it hadn't entered his learned head that perhaps she hadn't a wardrobe geared to take two weeks on a cruise ship in its stride. She wouldn't need much, for she was sensible enough to know that shore leave would be on a rota system and probably brief, but lying in bed mentally surveying the summer clothes she hadn't expected to wear again that year, she had come to the conclusion that they would require one or two additions. Cotton dresses and perhaps, although she was doubtful about this, a new evening dress. She should have asked about meals on board; did the nurses eat with the passengers or on their own? and surely if they did eat with everyone else, they would have to dress as they did? No one, she concluded, would want to eat his dinner opposite or beside a uniformed nurse. She closed her eyes, glad that she had decided what to do, and had then opened them again to review, hazily, her bank balance. There would be enough. She closed her eyes again and went to sleep.

Monday and Tuesday slid past at a great rate, she went off duty on Tuesday evening, late and tired and grumpy because Sister Moody had meanly taken an evening for herself and left her to work until nine o'clock, but late though it was there was something she had to do. She went first to Men's Medical and found Charlie still awake.

'Jist the gal I wanted,' he told her perkily. 'I'm going the day arter termorrer. Got a job, jist like yer said.'

Octavia settled silently on to the bed. 'Tell me about it,' she whispered. 'Is it in London? I hope it's not heavy work…'

He grinned at her, showing terrible teeth. 'Don't yer fret, lady—it's a real good job, 'andyman in a big 'ouse. I 'ain't seen the boss yet, only some gent 'o's acting for 'im. A real gent, too, coming ter fetch me an' all...'

Octavia frowned, 'Yes, but Charlie, you ought to know something about it first...'

'Not ter worry, Sister. Doctor Toms, 'e says 'e knows the boss personal and 'e's a real bloke.'

She looked at Charlie's face; it would never be youthful again, but at least it had filled out nicely and his eyes were bright and hopeful. She smiled and asked: 'How much are they going to give you?'

Charlie told her and he grinned again, as his bony frame seemed to swell with pride.

'Smashing, Charlie, the best of luck. I'm going away for a couple of weeks, but do let me know how you get on.'

They shook hands like old friends and Octavia slipped from the darkened ward and made her way to Women's Surgical; there was still Mrs Stubbs to say goodbye to.

That lady was sitting up in bed, her bedside light on, her spectacles on her nose, mending a pair of tights. 'That poor young nurse,' she explained, 'comes on duty and trips against one of those nasty trolleys and ruins her tights; I'm just catching the ladder before it gets too bad.' She chuckled gently. 'Night Sister won't be round for another half an hour.'

'Well, it's splendid to see you looking so fit, Mrs Stubbs. When are you going to your new job, and where is it?'

'Day after tomorrow, love, 'elping the 'ousekeeper, that's what I'm going ter do. The gent what's engaged me 'as several 'omes, so I don't rightly know where I'll be. That nice Mr Yates knows him, so I'm ever so 'appy. It's an ill wind that don't blow no one no good. I've been ever so 'appy 'ere, but it'll be nice to be doing something again.' She snipped a thread and glanced at Octavia. 'And you're off late? 'Ad a busy day, I'll be bound.'

'Well, so-so. I'm going away for a couple of weeks, so I'll say goodbye, Mrs Stubbs, but I hope I'll see you again; you must come and see us all, you know, once you're settled in.' She held out her hand and bent to kiss the elderly cheek. 'I'm so glad everything's turned out so well for you and I hope you'll love your job—whoever gets you is jolly lucky.'

And that was true, she thought, as she made her way to the Nurses' Home. Nowadays, nice cosy little women like Mrs Stubbs were few and far between, and she would be handy to have about the house, mending and ironing and doing a little plain cooking and baby-sitting on the side. Octavia wondered fleetingly if the family she was going to was a large one. She had forgotten to ask, not that Mrs Stubbs seemed to know much about it—nor had Charlie for that matter. It seemed strange, but then if Mr Yates and Doctor Toms vouched for them… She opened the sitting room door and went in to cries of: 'There you are—where have you been? It's half past nine… We saved some tea… Have you done your packing?'

She had decided to go home on Thursday afternoon and shop before she went; it seemed strange to hear everyone trooping off to breakfast the next morning and know that she was free to lie in bed if she wanted to. Not that she had the time for that; she bathed and dressed and got herself a sketchy meal in the little pantry at the end of the corridor and hurried out. Fenwick's, she had decided, or perhaps Wallis's, or even Dickins and Jones.

She spent a busy morning and an even busier afternoon; the shops were full of autumn clothes and cotton dresses were hard to find. The departments selling cruise clothes had plenty but at prices which hardly seemed justifiable for the brief hours she expected to spend off duty. She found two finally; not quite what she wanted, but she was clever with her needle and there would be time to alter them to suit herself. The evening dress was a good deal easier to find, indeed, the choice was so wide that she found it difficult to choose. She settled finally for a pastel patterned organza, very plainly cut and costing a good deal more than she had intended to pay, so that by way of righting this, she purchased a pair of gold sandals, flimsy things with high heels; it was only when she got back with them that she found herself wondering if they weren't quite practical for on board ship. 'But who wants to be practical?' she asked herself out loud. Probably she would spend most of her day in sensible lace-ups and a uniform.

She tried on the new outfits that evening before an audience of most of her friends, and everyone agreed that the sandals had been an absolute must with the new dress; such an expensive garment would have been ruined with anything less—besides, one might as well be hanged for a sheep as for a lamb. Octavia went to bed pleased with her day and tomorrow she would go home and tell her father about her temporary job. Probably he would forget all about it the moment she left the house, but she would send him a card from the first port of call just to remind him.

There was a letter for her in the morning, though she had no time to read it until she was in the train on the way to Alresford, and indeed she had quite forgotten it until the passenger opposite her in the carriage began to read a letter of his own. She opened the bulky envelope to discover that she was to report for duty at Southampton Docks at six o'clock on Friday evening. It went on to detail her duties, her free time and her salary; it also informed her of the itinerary—Malta, Athens, Rhodes, Alexandria, Sicily…it sounded marvellous provided she had a chance to go on shore, but that, it seemed, was left to the discretion of the senior ship's doctor. She folded the missive and put it back tidily in its envelope, hoping that that gentleman would be easy to work for and that there would be no dire emergency while she was on board. She was highly trained, skilled in theatre work, midwifery and children's ailments, as well as capable of dealing with the nastiest casualties, but there was always something… She shook off her apprehension, telling herself that she was twenty-seven years old and perfectly able to deal with anything which might come her way. 'And let's hope that the other nurses are friendly,' she told herself silently, 'as I suppose we see rather a lot of each other.' She reassured herself with the thought that it was only for a fortnight, anyway.

She had telephoned her father on the previous evening, but there was no one at the station. She took a taxi home and opened the front door calling: 'It's me, Father,' and Mrs Lovelace stuck her head round the kitchen door to say: 'Miss Octavia, what a surprise! I didn't know…will you be here for lunch? I was just going to dish up.'

Octavia put down her case. 'I telephoned Father yesterday—I expect he forgot to tell you, Mrs Lovelace. I'm just here until tomorrow afternoon, and don't worry about lunch, I'll have something cold.'

Mrs Lovelace looked shocked. 'Indeed you will not! I made a nice little steak and kidney pie for your father, there'll be enough for the two of you if I do some more veg. Just you go and see him while I see to it.'

Professor Lock was deeply engrossed in a book when she went in. He looked up briefly and murmured: 'Octavia—how very nice to see you,' and returned to his reading until she leaned over and took the book from him.

'Hullo, Father—I telephoned you yesterday evening, but I expect it slipped your mind. I'm going again tomorrow.'

'Your weekends seem to get shorter and shorter, my dear.'

'This isn't a weekend, my dear. It's only Thursday, but I thought I'd better let you know that I shall be away for a couple of weeks. I'm taking a temporary job as ship's nurse because they want someone in a hurry.'

He took the spectacles off his nose and looked at her. 'My dear child, I had no idea that you had lost your job at St Maud's!'

'I haven't, Father,' she smiled at him in a motherly fashion. 'Mr Yates, the Senior Consultant Surgeon, asked me if I would fill in for the nurse who's been taken ill. I'm to go to Southampton tomorrow and join the SS *Socrates* there. It's a Mediterranean cruise—I hope I'll see something of the places we'll visit.'

Her father brightened. 'Athens? Delightful, Octavia, quite delightful, there are several places which you must visit.'

'If I get shore leave,' she reminded him gently.

He waved an airy hand. 'Surely that will be granted if you particularly wish to see something…let me see…I must write a list of the more interesting monuments.'

'Yes, dear, and I'll do my best to look at every one of them.' Privately she thought it very unlikely that she would have the chance to see more than a modicum of them, but it was nice to see her absentminded parent so interested. She left him happily embarked on his list and went off to her room to get ready for lunch.

She told Mrs Lovelace all about it while she helped her dish up and then wrote down directions as to how she might be reached in an emergency, and Mrs Lovelace, while expressing her doubts about telephoning a ship in the middle of the sea, miles from anywhere, promised to carry them out if occasion should arise. 'Though Doctor

Dodds was here only last week,' she observed comfortably, 'having dinner with your pa, and he told me that he was in fine shape, Miss Octavia. But don't you worry, I'll look after him.'

Octavia spent the rest of the day re-packing her case, listening patiently to her parent's instructions as to what she should and should not see, deeming it a waste of time to point out to him that probably she would have no chance to see any one of them. They had their tea together in his study and presently she went along to the kitchen to cook their supper which Mrs Lovelace had so carefully prepared.

She spent the next morning visiting some of her numerous friends and after lunch bade her father goodbye, took a taxi to the station and began her journey to Southampton; not a long one, but it meant changing at Winchester and getting a taxi from the station to the docks.

She sat back in the cab as it made its way through the crowded streets feeling excited and faintly worried that she might not like the job, or worse, the people she was to work with wouldn't like her, but nothing of this showed on her face. She looked calm and very pretty in the coffee-coloured blouse and skirt with their matching suede jerkin that she had chosen to wear, under the mistaken impression that the outfit made her look older and rather staid. She could see the ship now, lying alongside the Customs building, she looked huge; and Octavia wondered if she would find her way round it easily. She would have to get hold of a plan and learn it off by heart.

There weren't many cars or taxis around, although there were men loading the ship and several figures going up and down the gang-ways. Octavia got out of the taxi and paid the driver and found a porter at her elbow almost at once. 'The *Socrates*?' he asked. 'Ship's company, miss?'

She supposed that was what she was, so she told him yes and found herself ushered through Customs with the minimum of fuss and with the porter still carrying her case, waved towards the aft gangway. There was an officer at the top, a nice, pleasant-faced man, with a wrinkled face and bright blue eyes, who gave her an enquiring look and waited for her to speak.

'Octavia Lock,' she told him in a matter-of-fact manner. 'I'm to replace the nurse who's gone off sick.'

He glanced at the papers in his hand. 'Welcome aboard, Miss Lock.' He turned to a passing steward. 'Take Nurse to her quarters, will you?' He dismissed her with a kindly nod. 'The other two are already aboard, so you'll be able to get acquainted before the doctors arrive.'

She followed the steward down two decks and then along a corridor lined with doors, crossed a foyer and plunged through a small door into another smaller passage. It was quite short and held only four doors, at the first of which the steward stopped and knocked. A voice told him to go in and he opened the door, put Octavia's case inside and stood aside to let her enter.

The cabin was quite large with two bunks against one wall and a third facing them. There was a good sized window, a dressing table, built-in cupboards and two chairs, over and above these there were two young women in the cabin. They turned to stare at Octavia as she stood just inside the door and she returned their look pleasantly, smiling while she studied them in her turn. The younger of the two was smiling at her from a round youthful face framed with soft light brown hair; she looked about twenty-two or so and was dressed rather untidily in a jersey dress which did nothing for her. Octavia took to her at once and her smile widened as the girl got to her feet and put out a hand. 'Hullo—I'm Mary Silver, the junior nurse. You're

Octavia Lock, aren't you? This is Joan Wise, she's the senior ship's nurse.'

Octavia transferred her gaze to the other occupant of the cabin; older than she had expected, well into her thirties, she imagined, with a handsome face exquisitely made up and platinum blonde hair which was just a shade too blonde. She was beautifully turned out, too, and the smile she gave Octavia was charming, only her eyes didn't smile. Octavia experienced the unpleasant feeling that she wasn't liked and dismissed the thought as fanciful as she exchanged greetings with her. If they were going to be together for the next two weeks, the quicker they got to like each other the better. Her good resolution was strained to its limit when Joan Wise said in a decided voice: 'The top bunk's yours; you're the newcomer, you see. You're senior to Mary but junior to me. I don't know what you were doing before you took this job, but I'm in charge—just as long as you remember that.'

Octavia murmured something or other and looked about her. It was a pity that she seemed to have exchanged Sister Moody for another of her kind, but that wouldn't really matter, probably once they were at sea, they would see little of each other than during sleeping hours. 'Will you tell me which drawer I may have and where I can hang my things?' she asked them both, but it was Mary who answered and showed her where they were. 'And here's the shower,' she opened a door and displayed the compact little place. 'If you like to unpack first, I expect Joan will explain duties and so on.'

They were all on duty each morning and took it in turns to be on duty in the afternoons, and provided there was nothing much to do, two of them would be free in the evenings. As for shore leave—well, that depended very much on the doctor. 'It's no good you expecting to go ashore each time we call somewhere,' Joan explained sharply. 'There's a rota and we take turns. I arrange it and he OKs it—I'm afraid you'll just have to accept what's offered. And of course if anything crops up, you'll probably have to do without your time off.'

She eyed Octavia's case. 'I hope you haven't brought too much with you—you'll be lucky if you get a chance to wear evening clothes more than a couple of times. We usually sunbathe in the afternoons when we're free, but you can do what you like; use the library or do some shopping or swim.' She added with a nasty little edge to her voice: 'Just remember you're not a passenger, that's all.'

Octavia gave her a cool glance. 'Oh, I won't do that. Do I fetch my uniform?'

'It'll be brought here. You'd better unpack. Mary and I are going down to the hospital, so come down there when you're ready and I'll show you round.'

Left to herself, Octavia put away her things, thankful that she hadn't brought a great deal with her, for there wasn't all that much space left for her. Mary, she reflected, would be pleasant enough, but she didn't think she was going to like Joan Wise. She seemed jealous of her authority, which was a bit silly, seeing that they were all three trained nurses, and Octavia suspected that if anyone was going short of their off duty it wouldn't be Sister Wise.

It didn't take her long to tidy away her wardrobe and presently she left the cabin, went back through the door and into the foyer, and studied the ship's plan on one of the walls. Sister Wise hadn't told her where the hospital was, but it couldn't be all that hard to find. It took a few moments to decide which was the front and which the back of the ship, and to discover that the staircases were numbered; it was just a question of finding the right staircase nearest the hospital, which was several decks below her.

She did rather well, meeting no one at all and taking careful note of where she was going. The hospital was clearly marked, with a waiting room for patients beside it. Octavia opened its door and went in, agreeably surprised to find that it looked very like St Maud's on a very small scale. She could hear voices coming from a half-opened door at the end of the passage, but she paused to peep in the doors on either side of her. The doctor's surgery on her right, and very nice too, beautifully fitted up and elegant to boot; the other door revealed a four-bedded ward and beyond it, another bigger ward. She closed the door and poked her pretty head round the next door—the duty room, much better than the office they had on Casualty at Maud's. She had reached the half-open door by now and pushed it wide. This was the theatre, small but otherwise the prototype of any hospital theatre, with a small anaesthetic room next to it and the scrub room leading from it. She was taken round it at leisure, giving her time to discover where everything was and ask all the questions she wanted to. They were in the anaesthetic room when a young man in slacks and a sweater joined them, to be introduced as Colin White, the junior doctor.

He shook Octavia's hand and beamed at her. 'I say, this is jolly,' he told her. 'I had no idea…' He stopped and went a little red in the face, then went on; 'I hear this is your first trip, so I hope you enjoy it. It's my sixth and Mary has been at it for several months, and Joan here is an old hand, aren't you, Joan?'

Sister Wise's eyes flashed, but she smiled thinly. 'Oh, a very old hand,' she repeated. 'Now run along, there's a good man, I've got to show Nurse Lock everything this afternoon; there won't be much time after today.'

He went reluctantly, stopped to ask Octavia if he might

show her round the ship later on and when she said yes, beamed more widely than ever.

They were on the point of leaving the hospital when Mary whispered: 'Oh, here's the boss.'

Octavia had turned back to read a notice she hadn't seen, but she looked round, curious to see if the senior doctor was as nice as Colin White appeared to be. He did indeed look nice, and very handsome—even more so than when she had seen him for the first time in Casualty. He advanced to meet them, in no hurry at all, looking faintly annoyed about something and when he saw her, frowning fiercely. Octavia, a forthright girl, ignored the frown.

'Well,' she exclaimed cheerfully, 'fancy meeting you again! Of course, now I think about it, you just had to be a doctor.'

CHAPTER THREE

OCTAVIA was aware that Joan Wise was staring at her; so was Mary, but Mary was smiling whereas Joan wasn't. As for the newcomer, his frown had deepened if anything so that she was tempted to add: 'You don't look at all pleased to see me.'

He didn't answer that; merely said formally: 'How do you do, Miss Lock,' and turned to Joan Wise, who gave him a dazzling smile and fluttered her eyelashes at him.

'We didn't expect you quite so soon,' she told him in what Octavia privately thought to be a ridiculously sugary voice. 'I've just been showing our new nurse round.'

His heavy-lidded eyes rested upon Octavia for a few seconds. 'Ah, yes—of course, although I'm sure she will have no difficulty in coping. She is Casualty Sister at St Maud's and is very experienced.'

Nicely said, approved Octavia silently; it was a pity that his tone had implied that she was not only experienced but no longer in the first flush of youth. Common sense reminded her that she wasn't, but what girl wants to be reminded that thirty isn't all that far off, even if she were as pretty as a picture? Octavia frowned in her turn and caught his eye; it was disconcerting to see a decided twinkle there.

He spoke to Mary next with a quiet casualness which

put that rather shy girl at her ease, and then turned to Octavia. 'Although we have met and I know your name, I think perhaps you won't know mine—van der Weijnen, Dutch. I should explain too that I am filling in for Doctor Blamey—he will be rejoining the ship when we return to Southampton.' He smiled at her briefly and added to Sister Wise: 'We are fortunate in having someone as experienced as yourself, Sister Wise, to guide us through any possible pitfalls.'

Octavia suppressed a smile. Anyone less likely to need guiding than the new doctor she had yet to meet, and as for Joan Wise...she was much more likely to give anyone a good push into a pit and then stand on its edge and point out their error. She stood quietly while the doctor and Sister Wise exchanged small talk and presently, dismissed by a nod from Sister Wise, accompanied Mary up on deck to see what was going on.

'She's got her claws into him,' observed Mary. 'She's all of thirty-five, you know, and all the older men are married—I don't know if this one is, but I thought he was rather nice when we met him the other day, but of course he's only with us for a fortnight.' She looked anxiously at Octavia, 'Do you think that's time enough?'

'Plenty, as long as he's willing.' Octavia paused and went on thoughtfully, 'But I shouldn't think he'd be all that easy...'

'He was super, calling you Sister like that when Joan had just said Nurse in that scornful voice. I've not been a Sister, only a staff nurse; I expect you're frightfully clever...'

'Lord no—just luck. You know how a job comes up and there's no one much for it? I was just lucky.'

'He said you were very clever,' persisted Mary.

'Oh, he was just being pleasant—making conversation.

In any case, we only met the once and that for a very short time—he brought someone into Casualty one evening and I happened to be on duty.' Octavia leaned her elbows on the ship's rail and gazed down at the activities on the dock below. 'Gosh, aren't they busy? Are we free now or do we have to take duty in turns?'

'Joan will tell us presently; she arranges the duties and she hates anyone to ask to have them changed, but if she's in a good mood, I expect she'll let you go ashore if she doesn't want to.'

Octavia turned to look at her companion. 'Tell me, Mary, what sort of girl left? I mean, before Suzy was appointed in her place?'

'Oh, very quiet and kind of earnest; she always did exactly what Joan told her to do and she never once asked for time off to go ashore or anything like that, and she never went to any of the cabarets or went dancing when she was off duty…'

'I have a horrid feeling,' observed Octavia meditatively, 'that I'm going to be a square peg in a round hole.'

She had no chance to test her theory for the moment, however; Sister Wise had disappeared for the time being, leaving Mary and herself to make sure that everything was exactly as it should be before the first of the passengers came on board the next day. It wasn't until the following morning that she found time to discuss their duty hours with them, because she had come to bed long after the two of them were asleep. 'Having a go at charming the boss,' Mary had observed over breakfast. 'She looks much younger by electric light…'

Octavia had laughed at that. 'Mary, if I didn't know what a nice girl you were I might think you were being catty!' She poured second cups of coffee for them both. 'Besides, Doctor van der Weijnen is old enough to take care of himself. Which reminds me—he's a professor, too—I remember seeing it in the Casualty Book.'

Mary bit into a slice of toast. 'Whatever made him take on this job? You don't think he's hiding from someone, or perhaps…'

'Lord no, Mary—you heard what he said; he's filling in for Doctor Blamey—possibly they're friends and he's got a couple of weeks' holiday.' She pushed back her chair. 'Oughtn't we to start thinking of this boat drill? It's almost time.'

It was hard to take boat drill seriously. Octavia, swamped in a life-jacket, was inspected by the Captain and a little posse of officers, among whom were Doctor van der Weijnen and Colin White, who winked at her. She didn't look at the Dutchman—easy enough, for her eyes were on a level with his tie, although she found herself tempted to glance up at him. Leave that to our Joan, she told herself severely, and obedient to orders tested the whistle dangling from her life-jacket.

They dispersed for coffee after that and Sister Wise joined them, notebook and pen in hand. 'The duty hours,' she explained loftily. 'Eight o'clock until two o'clock and on call from ten o'clock at night until eight o'clock the following morning. Then from two o'clock until ten o'clock in the evening, the third rota is on call from eight o'clock until two o'clock and then free for the rest of the day—which means that on every third day we're each free from two o'clock and on each third night one of us will be on call. Should there be a case during the night, whoever is on call must endeavour to cope by herself; we can't have all three of us up all night. Of course, these times are changed when we are in port; we'll settle that later.' She fixed Octavia with a cold stare. 'I hope you're quite satisfied, Octavia?' Not at all what Mary had told her—in fact a dreadful muddle, decided Octavia; such airy-fairy duty hours would end in confusion.

'It sounds fine. I expect we have to do a bit of give and take between us?'

'Naturally, but do understand that I am the one who arranges the duty hours.'

The first passengers arrived in the afternoon and the great ship, filling itself slowly with excited people, took on a holiday atmosphere. Octavia, her chores done, stood with Mary on deck and watched them come on board; mostly couples, and most of those not so very young, but there was a sprinkling of younger men and women too and several family parties in splendid spirits, and to her surprise, a number of very small babies.

'There'll be quite a few people travelling on their own,' Mary told her. 'There's a party for them all tomorrow evening so they can get to know each other.'

'I don't think I'd like to come alone. Do we go to dinner tonight?'

'Rather—we sit at different tables and help the conversation, though no one needs any help after the first day. Have you got something pretty to wear? Tomorrow we'll be in uniform—perhaps sooner if anyone's ill tonight.'

Octavia turned to look at her. 'You're a cheerful little thing, aren't you? The weather's lovely. I shouldn't think anyone would realise that we're moving, let alone bobbing up and down, and surely they're all too interested to think about being ill.'

'Well, yes,' Mary agreed, 'I've never known anyone be ill on the first night. Look, there's the boss coming up the gangway. He's very handsome, isn't he? Our Joan's going to get some stiff competition.' Mary giggled. 'I say, why don't you cut her out? You're ever so pretty, Octavia. I bet you could if you tried.'

Octavia turned away from the rail. 'I'm not in the least interested in him,' she declared briskly, and knew as she said it that there was no truth in the remark.

The first few days slid away. There wasn't much to do; a sprained ankle, a few cases of seasickness, brought on, Octavia considered, by apprehension, a handful of cuts and bruises, and that was all. The weather, now that they had rounded Cape St Vincent, was glorious and very warm; there would be several cases of sunburn later. In the meantime, the three of them took their free time during the day and slept without interruption each night. Octavia had acquired a light tan which set off her white uniform very nicely and made her prettier than ever. She was popular at her table in the restaurant too, and much in demand for dancing in the evening when she was off duty. If she had been a passenger and not a ship's nurse, she could have had a simply splendid time. As it was, she was pleasant to everyone without making any attempt to become especially friendly, indeed her behaviour was exemplary so that Sister Wise had no fault to find with her, and Mary, spending as much of her free time with Colin as she could, wanted to know anxiously if Octavia was enjoying herself. And Doctor van der Weijnen, presiding over the small morning surgery, lifted his head from the papers on his desk long enough to enquire if she had settled in nicely. She assured him in a cool voice that she had and was surprised when he went on: 'I haven't seen you dancing a great deal—perhaps you don't enjoy it?'

'Every bit as much as you do, Doctor van der Weijnen,' said Octavia tartly.

'Perhaps I failed to see you…' His voice was bland.

'I shouldn't be surprised. There are some quite beautiful girls on board and you dance with them all, I imagine.'

He was looking down at the desk, his face turned away from her. 'Ah—yes, in the line of duty, Octavia.'

'Oh, pooh,' said Octavia with a complete disregard for manners. 'Shall I fetch the next patient in? Mrs Summers, complaining of earache.'

She was on duty that afternoon too; Joan Wise had some mysterious meeting which necessitated her being free and she had asked Octavia to stand in for her, in a voice which clearly expected her to do so without comment. So after lunch Octavia went back to the surgery, did a few little chores and then went to look out of the porthole. The sea looked wonderful, its rich blue paling towards the distant African coast on the horizon. She would have liked to be on deck, looking her fill instead of standing there doing nothing.

But she wasn't to do nothing for long; it wasn't time for surgery, but passengers could come at any time if it was necessary, and the short, stout man at the door obviously considered it was. 'I've got sunburn,' he told her. 'My back's killing me—you'll have to give me something, Nurse.'

Octavia moved to the desk and drew a card towards her. 'Yes, of course. May I have your name, please?'

'Love.' He leered at her. 'And I get a good few jokes made about it, I can tell you. Shall I take my shirt off?'

He had come a little nearer, bringing with him a strong aroma of spirits. She said calmly: 'Presently, Mr Love; the doctor will want to have a look at it…'

Mr Love came even nearer. 'Pretty little thing, aren't you?' he said, and hiccoughed loudly. A remark which made Octavia, five feet eight in her bare feet, smile involuntarily, which was a pity, because he took this as a sign of encouragement and slid an arm round her waist.

Octavia removed it. Casualty had produced enough patients of his type to leave her unstartled and quite capable of dealing with him. She frowned a little when he gripped her even more tightly, and said sharply: 'Let me go at once, Mr Love!'

An unnecessary warning; Doctor van der Weijnen's voice from the doorway sounded unruffled but icily commanding. 'Nurse can attend to you far more easily if you do as she asks, Mr—er—Love.' His voice was still icy when he asked her: 'What is wrong with our patient, Nurse?'

'Sunburn,' said Octavia testily, 'although I'm uncertain as to where at the moment.'

'Then shall we ask Mr Love to remove his shirt so that I may look?'

Mr Love, cowed, but still hopelessly inebriated, did as he was bid, exposing a back and chest closely resembling all the fiery colour of a freshly boiled lobster. The doctor tut-tutted gently as he examined him, made a few wise-sounding remarks about the good sense of not overexposing the human body to the sun's rays and desired Octavia to fetch a soothing ointment which he directed her to apply while he watched. She was handing Mr Love his shirt when that gentleman, a little more himself by now, remarked slyly in a still slurred voice: 'Apologies—didn't know I was trespassing on your preserves, Doc.' He winked and nodded at him and received a glacial stare in return. 'I beg your pardon?'

He was impervious to the dangerously quiet voice. 'Granted, Doc—we all fancy a pretty girl, and I daresay this young lady knows which side her bread is buttered.' He chuckled. 'You must have plenty of opportunity, the pair of you.'

Octavia, her cheeks very pink, went on tidying up, neither looking nor speaking. It was the doctor who replied in a nastily silky voice: 'I must ask you to apologise to Nurse for that remark, Mr Love. We both realise that you are not quite yourself, so I will make no mention of slander…'

Mr Love's little eyes almost popped from his head. 'Slander? No offence meant, I'm sure—my little joke, you know. I'm sure I apologise to Nurse if I've said something I shouldn't…'

'You have,' he was reminded softly, 'and I do most strongly advise you not to do so again. As to your sunburn, if you will apply this lotion each night and morning I think you will find that you will be cured within a day or so. If not, would you come back here?'

Octavia, watching Mr Love take the bottle, was privately of the opinion that nothing short of being burned to a crisp would bring Mr Love back. She closed the door gently and looked at the doctor's broad back as he sat at the desk. His sharp: 'Well, have you nothing better to do than stare?' made her jump.

She bit back the pert retort on the tip of her tongue and said instead: 'Thank you for dealing with Mr Love,' and then, rather severely: 'I am quite capable of coping with such patients, though.'

He didn't look up from his writing. 'I had noticed that,' he observed drily.

The remark annoyed her, but she could think of no answer, so she asked: 'Am I to call you Doctor or Professor?'

'Doctor will do very nicely, Octavia.' She was at the door on her way out when he said very softly: 'A man should look after his own, you know.'

She wondered what he had meant by that as she made her way to the duty room. After all, he was only standing in for the permanent ship's doctor, so he could hardly consider the three nurses and his junior doctor to be his own. She dismissed the thought and set about ruling up the books and making a note in her neat handwriting about Mr Love.

There was nothing to do for the rest of the afternoon. Octavia drank her tea and wished the hours away until evening surgery, that wasn't busy either and Colin took it; of his senior there was no sign. It wasn't until she was going off duty that she encountered him on the stairs on his way down to second dinner, very handsome in his dress uniform, but beyond a casual good evening he had nothing to say, so that she paused deliberately in front of him.

'Have a pleasant evening, Professor van der Weijnen—there are some very pretty girls on board.'

'As you have already remarked only a few hours ago, Octavia. Be sure that I have marked down the prettiest of them. And you? A pleasant evening too, I hope?'

'By the time I've had dinner there won't be much of an evening left.' She added with a bright smile: 'I don't mind in the least.'

He only nodded, wished her a cool goodnight and went on his way, leaving her to go and eat her dinner, go to the library and fetch a book before going to the cabin. She was asleep when the other two came in.

She was free the next morning and on call that night, so she spent the morning sunbathing in a quiet corner of one of the decks and after a quick swim in one of the pools and a buffet lunch, she dressed and hung over the rails watching the very last of the distant African coast slide away over the horizon. She had missed Gibraltar, although the ship hadn't called there. Probably she would miss Sicily, too; Joan Wise hadn't said a word about which of them was to be free to go ashore there. She had changed Octavia's hours several times already on the pretext that she herself had various meetings to attend and someone would have to fill in for her. Octavia had expected that she would be given more free time to make up for this, but nothing had been said—perhaps, she thought hopefully, she would be given shore leave after all.

She had her tea presently and then lay in the sun writing to her father, then when the pool was almost empty while the passengers were dressing for the evening, she had another swim. She was free until ten o'clock, so she put on a pale cotton evening dress and presently, in Joan Wise's company, went down to the restaurant, where they parted, Sister Wise to join Colin and herself to the table for six where she sat when she was off duty. Its occupants greeted her with cries of pleasure. She had been missed, they declared, and proceeded to make much of her rather noisily during the meal and at its end swept her along with them to one of the dance floors, declaring that she must have at least half an hour's dancing before she left them. They passed the table at which the doctor was presiding and he gave her an unsmiling look as they did so, but as he so seldom smiled at her, she didn't allow this to worry her; indeed, she felt pleasure in the fact that she was wearing a becoming dress and looked at least as eye-catching as any girl there.

It was like being Cinderella, she thought ruefully as she slipped away from the dancers just before ten o'clock, and after checking at the hospital and taking over from Mary, the pair of them went along to their cabin. A dull duty, Mary told her between yawns. 'Nothing happens, does it?' she observed. 'You'll get a sound sleep, Octavia—getting up at night happens once in a lifetime on board ship. What a pity Joan hasn't told us our duty for tomorrow—I can't think why not, we always know days ahead. That's a lovely dress…you're so pretty.'

'Pooh,' said Octavia, 'and even if I were, little you'd care, with Colin making eyes at you.'

Mary wrapped her dressing gown round her small person. 'I know—I do hope I don't get shore leave tomorrow; he's on duty, you see, and if I am too, it would be super—there'll be no one much on board, you see.'

Octavia made suitably sympathetic sounds and wondered if she would be lucky enough to get ashore. Probably not; she was sure by now that Joan Wise didn't like her. They finished their preparations for bed and then lay, gossiping gently, until first one and then the other fell asleep. They neither of them heard Sister Wise come in a good deal later.

The high-sounding persistent bleep, muffled by Octavia's pillow, dragged her back from sleep. She whipped from her bunk, cast her dressing gown round her shoulders and went soundlessly from the cabin. There was a telephone in the passage outside and before she had time to speak into it, Doctor van der Weijnen's voice spoke into her ear: 'Good girl. Dress and come down to cabin 336; we've an ectopic on our hands.'

She was there in three minutes flat; moreover, she had wakened no one as she had raced into her clothes—no stockings and her hair tied back in a ponytail; no one would notice her bare legs and her hair would be tucked away under her theatre cap, anyway. She looked calm and efficient and wide awake, which was a good thing, because Mrs Bluett in cabin 336 was in a bad way, shocked and pale and in pain. Doctor van der Weijnen was drawing up an injection as Octavia joined him and he didn't look up.

'I have explained to Mrs Bluett that she must come to theatre so that we may help her immediately—I have already spoken to her husband. The two sick bay orderlies will be here in a moment with the stretcher—can you manage on your own? They'll be in theatre to give you a hand, of course, and Colin will be giving the anaesthetic.' He looked up suddenly and smiled, a smile of charm and complete confidence in himself and her, so that she smiled back and said matter-of-factly:

'Of course. Do you want me here or shall I go and get things ready.'

'Go now, if you will.'

'What about a transfusion?'

He gave her an appreciative glance. 'I've cross-matched with her husband—Colin will see to that before we start. Now run along.'

Octavia ran, glad that she had learned the geography of the great ship and didn't have to hesitate at all. She had the key to the hospital with her and left the door unlocked before she hurried through to the tiny anaesthetic room. There were several things to see to before she could lay up; a bed to prepare in the ward, a quick check to make sure that everything was just so and in its right place, equipment to be plugged in, sterilisers to be switched on. She did everything methodically and quickly, her mind racing ahead of her hands so that not a second should be lost.

She had everything nicely ready by the time Colin arrived with Mrs Bluett and the two orderlies, even her husband, almost as pale and apprehensive as his wife, lying ready on the couch in the surgery, waiting to give his blood. And a few minutes later Doctor van der Weijnen came quietly in, looking so placid that one would imagine that he was in the habit of operating at two o'clock in the morning. But Octavia really had no time to think about that, she was perfectly able to manage on her own; the orderlies were reliable and she knew her work well, but she would have to use her wits. She threaded her needles with steady hands and when the doctor had scrubbed, signed to one of the orderlies to tie him into his gown.

The whole, urgent operation went off without a hitch.

Doctor van der Weijnen worked fast and surely, showing no sign of temperament or impatience and obligingly helping himself to the instruments when Octavia was occupied in holding retractors or cutting gut as he tied. And when he had finished and made sure that his patient was as comfortable as possible in one of the hospital beds, he remained to set up the drip himself while Colin saw to blood pressure, pulse and the general condition of Mrs Bluett, leaving Octavia free to return to theatre and start on the clearing. In this she was ably assisted by her two helpers, so that presently she was able to leave them to the washdown while she cleaned the instruments, got them into the steriliser and began on the sharps.

By now she was thoroughly awake and rather enjoying herself. She had forgotten what a lot of extra work one had without the aid of disposable equipment and ready sterilised packs coming from the CSSD each day. Here, on board, it all had to be done by the nurse or nurses on duty. She whistled softly while she worked, went to check on Mr Bluett, waiting patiently in the waiting room, shared a pot of tea with him while he talked himself into a happier frame of mind and then went back to her work, reassuring him that she would remain for the rest of the night with his wife, and that he could go back to his cabin when he had seen her.

She finished finally, tidied herself as well as she was able and went along to the ward. Both doctors were still there, but it was Doctor van der Weijnen who asked her if she was finished and quite ready to take over. 'There's no hurry,' he told her kindly. 'Have you had a cup of tea?—I asked them to see to it. Mrs Bluett is quite all right, if you will come here a minute I will give you my written instructions…'

Both men went presently, with instructions that they

were to be called if she felt any doubt about her patient's condition. 'And I shall be along before you go off duty,' promised Doctor van der Weijnen. He paused at the door. 'Thank you, Octavia, you managed splendidly.' He smiled gently at her. 'If you need anyone, call me—Colin needs some sleep, he's on duty in the morning and on call for the rest of the day.' He glanced back to the quiet woman on the bed. 'Mrs Bluett should sleep on that Pethidene until morning—it's morning now, isn't it?'

He closed the door quietly and Octavia was left to sit down beside her patient and think about the eventful night. There were almost four hours left before she would be relieved, and she remembered with regret that the ship was due at Palermo about midday. It seemed unlikely that she would get ashore even if she made do with an hour or two's sleep. She sat, her mind empty of thoughts, until Mrs Bluett stirred and she could begin on the morning chores to make her comfortable. She had almost finished when Doctor van der Weijnen came back. His 'good morning' was pleasant and he saw at a glance that she needed help to get Mrs Bluett up against her pillows. This done, he listened to Octavia's report, expressed satisfaction at his patient's condition and very much to her surprise told her to go and get some breakfast.

'But I can't,' she told him flatly. 'I'm on duty.'

'I shall be here for half an hour,' he observed, and as she went rather reluctantly to the door, pointed out that her hair was coming down.

Octavia cast him an outraged look. 'It's never been up,' she observed tartly. 'You told me to be quick, if you remember. And I had to gallop the length of the ship as well!' She shut the door on his chuckle.

He went as soon as she returned, with a few instructions, briefly given, and soon afterwards she handed over to Mary. She was on the point of going off duty when Joan Wise came in. 'I shall have to take morning surgery,' she remarked shortly, and then turned to Octavia with a brief: 'Well?'

Octavia related the night's happenings and Mary interrupted to ask: 'How long have you been up, Octavia?' and when she told her, Sister Wise said at once:

'Mary, you'll be on duty until one o'clock today, then go on call. Octavia, get some sleep and take over from one o'clock until eight this evening. I shall be going ashore.'

'But that's not fair...' Octavia hushed Mary's shocked voice with a little smile and Joan Wise said:

'I'm the senior and I have first choice. After all, Octavia, you weren't called until two o'clock. You must have had some sleep. I'll take over at eight o'clock this evening and stay until midnight. Mary can take over for the rest of the night and you, Octavia, can do duty from eight o'clock until two in the afternoon.'

She smiled thinly and went along to the waiting room, leaving Mary to say: 'How mean can you get? You've been up almost all night and you could easily have turned nasty and insisted on having help. The least she could do would be to let you go ashore this afternoon!'

'Never mind, Mary, it doesn't matter all that much. After all, I'm only temporary and I suppose she feels she can make use of me, though I've never met anyone who could muddle the duty hours so appallingly as she does. It's easy enough with three of us.'

'Yes, but you see she doesn't share the duties fairly—at least, it looks as though she does, but she gets out of an awful lot.'

Octavia yawned. 'Don't worry about it, Mary—I'm going to say goodbye to Mrs Bluett and then I'm off to bed. Who'll wake me?'

'I will—Tom or William will be here, so I'll be able to leave for a minute or two.'

Octavia was going slowly up the stairs when she bumped into Doctor van der Weijnen once more. 'Off duty?' he wanted to know. 'You'll be free when you've had some sleep?'

She saw no reason to tell him otherwise than yes; it really couldn't matter to him what she did with her free time, even when it had been cut to a bare minimum. She wished him goodbye in a mumbling voice because she was almost asleep already, and took herself off to a shower and bed. She was on the point of sleep when she remembered that if she had gone on deck, she would at least have had a glimpse of Sicily even if she never set foot on it.

It seemed only minutes before Mary's excited voice dragged her back from sleep. Octavia pulled the sheet over her head. 'Go away,' she mumbled.

'It's one o'clock,' said Mary.

Octavia cast the sheet off her person and sat bolt upright, 'I'm on at once—I'll be late, why didn't you call me…?'

'Because I was told not to—not until now.' Mary drew a deep breath. 'Guess what, Joan's on duty instead of you.'

'Why? In heaven's name, whatever's happened?'

Mary grinned cheerfully. 'Oh, nothing—nothing at all. Only you've got shore leave until six o'clock. You have to go on duty at eight o'clock and stay until midnight—I'm to relieve you.'

'I'm to go ashore?' Octavia scrambled down, yawning prodigiously, and then stretched her arms widely, her hair a wild mass over her shoulders.

'Oh, Octavia, you're so pretty!'

She was already searching in a drawer for her undies. 'Stuff, Mary—and even if I were, what would that matter to you when your Colin has no eyes for anyone but you—did you get a chance to see something of him?' And before Mary could answer: 'You can't do night duty—you're on call.'

'Well, yes, but the boss said I could do what I liked as long as I was on board, I don't have to stay in uniform, so it'll be the same as being off duty. I told the steward to bring you some tea and a sandwich.'

'Angel!' declared Octavia, and dived into the bathroom. 'I'll do the same for you one of these days.'

She put on a cotton shirtwaister, a pale Liberty print with a modest neckline and short sleeves because she was fairly sure that the people of Sicily didn't care for bare arms and shorts, especially in their churches, and she intended to visit several. Her hair she tied back with a thick tortoiseshell slide and then slid her feet into sandals while she munched and swallowed, fearful of losing a second of precious time. She had to waste a few frustrating moments searching for her sunglasses, then ran through the deserted ship down to the lower deck where there was a gangway aft for the ship's personnel. She took the last flight of stairs at a gallop and turned the corner, to stop short. Doctor van der Weijnen was blocking the open door which led on to the deck and the gangway beyond.

CHAPTER FOUR

OCTAVIA let out her breath on a long sigh. The doctor hadn't moved one inch to let her pass and his: 'Not so fast, Octavia,' seemed to confirm her worst suspicions.

'It was a mistake'—her voice was wooden with disappointment. 'I'm on duty after all—I thought it was too good to be true.'

He said to no one in particular: 'I wonder why women jump to conclusions? Of course you're not on duty. I—er—arranged with Sister Wise to allow you time off.' He continued blandly, 'When I pointed out that you were due your usual off-duty she was persuaded to agree with me.'

Octavia eyed him doubtfully. 'Well, that's very kind of you—if you're sure it's all right…'

'Perfectly all right.' He put out an arm and plucked her through the door and across the deck and on to the gangway, and she, only too willing to put the problem of Sister Wise behind her, ran down it and then turned round as she reached the quayside, to find him right behind her.

'Oh, I thought you were still on the ship and I forgot to say how very grateful I am. I'm a bit excited…'

He stared down at her, massive and relaxed in his white uniform. 'The car's just across here,' he said to surprise her, and took her arm. He eyed her dress with approval. 'I see you're most suitably dressed; despite tactful suggestions, the ladies *will* wear sleeveless dresses and shorts.'

She glowed with pleasure. 'Oh, well...but aren't you on duty?' A silly question, for Colin was, and the two of them wouldn't be on and off together.

He smiled as though he had read her thoughts. They were strolling across the quay, past the gay little pony carts with their painted wheels and decorated ponies, to where several cars stood waiting.

He stopped beside a small Fiat, battered and hard-worked, and opened its door with a flourish. 'I'm assured that it goes like a bomb. Just as long as it doesn't explode like one!'

He crammed himself in beside her and switched on the engine, and Octavia, in a quite bewildered state of mind, asked: 'Yes, but am I going with you? I'd planned to walk and then get a bus to Monreale...did you mean to give me a lift?'

'Yes.' He gave her an enchanting smile and slid the little car between the other vehicles surrounding it. 'We have about four hours. Is there anything you especially wanted to see?'

'You mean I'm to go with you—all the afternoon?'

'If you can put up with a staid, middle-aged companion, yes.'

She sounded indignant. 'You're not—staid or middle-aged. Why, the women flock round you!'

He grinned. 'Had you noticed? But don't be deceived—it's their ailments they're interested in, not me.' They were driving down the street leading to the city and he wasn't hurrying. 'But I am middle-aged—almost forty—and I am staid, as befits a widower with a daughter of nine.'

Octavia choked back surprise and said levelly: 'Forty

isn't even middle-aged, and I expect having a daughter keeps you young.'

'Excellent Octavia—always ready with the right answer.' He sounded faintly mocking and she felt her cheeks warm, but he didn't seem to notice. They had entered the city now and he pulled in to the side of a busy street and stopped. 'Just across the road there is a delightful Palatine chapel built in the Arabian style. Would you like to see it?'

The chapel was set in a surprisingly quiet little cloister and garden where lemon trees, growing miraculously from the dry dusty soil, shaded narrow stone paths. And inside, although it was a small, bare building, there was the same peace. Octavia savoured the age-old atmosphere as they strolled through it and was thankful that her companion was silent. Indeed, it wasn't until they were in the garden again, making for the iron gate which separated it from the outside, modern world, that he spoke. 'Quite beautiful, isn't it—I daresay you know of it, but if I can answer any questions…?'

She began asking them at once and listened to his deep voice explaining about mediaeval art, the various peoples who had occupied the island, and the Norman influence, until he said: 'I'm prosing on and there is so much more to see.' He took her arm to cross the road. 'I think the cathedral at Monreale next—well worth a visit—you like architecture?'

'Yes, but nothing too modern. I like places to have a history.' She looked about her as they went with unexpected speed through the outskirts of Palermo, gained the countryside and started climbing towards Monreale, visible ahead of them with its cathedral towering above its roofs.

'You've been here before, Doctor van der Weijnen?'

'Yes. My name is Lucas.'

'Oh, but I can't…that is, you're a professor too.' She hadn't meant to say anything as foolish as that, but it was a little hard to explain.

'I see that you are determined not to allow me to forget my middle age.' He launched the car at a narrow gap between two overladen lorries and shot ahead once more.

Octavia laughed. She was beginning to enjoy herself very much; he was a dear, bad-tempered sometimes and inclined to be arrogant, but he had a sense of humour. 'If it helps, I'm twenty-seven myself… Lucas.'

'I know. You are also a strikingly handsome young woman. I'm surprised that you aren't married—or at least engaged.' His voice held a faint note of enquiry and she answered readily enough.

'I've not liked anyone quite well enough.' She twisted round in her seat to admire the view behind them. 'What a super view there must be from Monreale.'

'Indeed there is.' The little car was climbing valiantly and presently took the last turn into the town, houses climbing the hill alongside the road while on the other side the ground tumbled sharply down towards Palermo and the sea. 'We'll leave the car in the town and walk back here, if you like.'

The town was old and crumbling and full of life, with people sitting at little iron tables drinking and talking and the streets full of traffic and tourists. The cathedral stood at one side of a large square full of little stalls and the doctor drove slowly round it, past the ancient building, to park in an open space beyond, and then walked her back towards the cathedral entrance, not hurrying so that she had time to linger at the various stalls as they went. 'We'll shop later, if you like,' he told her obligingly, and ushered her into the vast dimness of the cathedral.

There was a great deal to see. Octavia was thankful

that they weren't one of any of the parties of tourists being shown round; she would never have remembered half of what the guides were saying and Lucas, even if he didn't know as much as they did, proved himself a tireless answerer of questions. She craned her lovely neck to get a better view of the ceiling, peered at richly decorated chapels and admired the paintings, then followed her companion to the cloisters where they wandered around in the hot sunshine, not saying much, while she wondered about him being a widower and having a small daughter. He would be a rather nice father, she decided, and was startled when he asked: 'I wonder what you're thinking, Octavia? You look so very serious,' and she answered him although she hadn't meant to:

'About your little daughter.'

'Berendina?'

'Is that her name? How pretty. You must miss her when you're away from home.'

It was disappointing when he said nothing but a laconic yes to this remark; she had hoped to hear more about him, and now, instead of that, it was his turn. Over a long cold drink at one of the little bars close to the cathedral, he began to question her himself, and it was done so skilfully that she had told him quite a lot before she realised what he was about.

'And why are you called Octavia?' he wanted to know.

'It was a joke. You see, my parents had been married quite some time before I was born, long enough for them to have had at least seven children, so they called me Octavia—besides, I was born on the eighth of August.'

'So you were the first and are the last?'

'Yes. My mother died ten years ago and my father is a Professor of Physics—he's retired now, but he still lectures and works at home.'

'And where is home?' He had slipped the question in so quietly that she barely noticed it.

'Alresford—quite a small town north of Southampton. It's not too far from London and I go home very often.' It was then that she realised that she was talking about herself far too much. She finished her drink and remarked brightly: 'What a very busy town this is.'

He made no attempt to ask her any more questions but suggested that they should stroll back to the edge of the town and look at the view, and once there they stood looking around them, letting the groups of tourists pass and re-pass, and presently, when the street was almost empty again, the doctor produced a very small camera and took photos, first of the various views and then of Octavia. 'Let me take one of you?' she asked him. 'You can give it to Berendina.'

So she took photos too until he declared that if they wanted to see anything else they would have to go on. They walked back to the car and went back down the hill towards Palermo. 'There's not much time left,' observed Lucas, 'but I think we can manage Bagheria and tea somewhere.'

Bagheria when they reached it proved enchanting. Octavia, listening to the doctor telling her the bald outlines of the history of the magnificent villa built by the Branciforti Princes of Burera and the extravagances of the Prince of Palagonia, wished she could have stayed for days. Finally he took her hand and marched her back to the car, exclaiming: 'I've never met a girl with such a curiosity about places. You will have to come again—and we've only scratched the tip of Sicily, you know.'

'And I'm not likely to come again,' Octavia pointed out soberly.

His comfortable 'Oh, I don't know about that,' didn't

really reassure her, but she cheered up when he stopped at an hotel and ordered tea. A quite substantial one too, for which she was thankful; her snatched lunch seemed a long while ago. She ate with appetite, enjoying the sandwiches and anchovy toast and little creamy cakes, remarking naïvely as she polished off the last one: 'I had no idea that they had tea like us—I mean the English, of course. I daresay you don't in Holland.'

He smiled at her across the elegant little table. He might have been forgiven for telling her that they didn't, that the meal had been provided for her benefit and at a considerable expense to himself, but his nature was as generous as his powerful body; it never entered his head to do so. He agreed placidly to her observations, agreed that English teatime was a pleasant institution and suggested that they should be going back to the ship.

They had ten minutes to spare after he had paid for the car; they spent it happily touring the stalls, doing a brisk trade to returning passengers. Octavia bought a little wooden model of a pony cart and her companion, smiling a little at her delight over the dolls dressed in a variety of Sicilian costumes, bought two and gave one to her, one for Berendina. 'A souvenir,' he told her, 'of a very pleasant afternoon.'

'Oh, it was,' agreed Octavia warmly. 'I had no idea…' She went a little pink and changed the sentence to 'that Palermo was so lovely,' quite failing to see the amusement in the doctor's eyes. 'But you haven't a souvenir,' she pointed out.

He glanced at his watch. 'You are mistaken, I have—tucked away out of sight. I shall enjoy it when I have forgotten everything else.'

She looked mystified and then concluded that as he had been there before, it was probably something he treasured—a gift from his dead wife perhaps. She said cheerfully: 'It's time to go, isn't it?' and slipped up the gangway ahead of him. On deck she thanked him once more before going below to the cabin. 'You've been very kind,' she told him. 'I don't mind if I can't go ashore anywhere else.'

He opened his eyes. 'Not Athens?'

She smiled resolutely, 'I can't expect everything, and it won't be my turn. I'll be on duty tomorrow.'

And she was quite right, of course. An ill-tempered Joan Wise, hardly bothering to speak to her, told her shortly that she would be on duty from eight o'clock the next morning until four o'clock that afternoon and then on call that night. Octavia was disappointed, but she had expected it; she changed for the evening in a defiant mood, although she barely had time to go to the restaurant and have her dinner at the first sitting before changing once again into uniform. Of the doctor there was no sign; she took over from a tight-lipped Sister Wise, and later received her instructions from Colin and set about the various small tasks she had been left to do. Mrs Bluett slept peacefully; she was making an entirely successful recovery and already looked astonishingly better. At midnight Mary came to relieve her, bubbling over with the news that Doctor van der Weijnen had been dancing with Joan Wise for most of the evening, an interesting statement which for some reason annoyed Octavia very much. She dismissed it as childish and asked:

'Mary, you're sure you'll be all right? Don't you want to go ashore in the morning? I could come on early…'

Mary shook her head. 'I'm going to do what you did,' she confided, 'only Colin is taking me as soon as I've had breakfast and changed—just for an hour or two. He's on duty at four o'clock. We'll have lunch somewhere and I can go to bed when we get back.' She looked up from the chart she was studying. 'What are you going to do.'

'Well, nothing. I'm on till four o'clock and the ship sails at seven, doesn't she? Perhaps I'll just dash down the gangway and walk round the passenger terminal.' Then with an attempt at gaiety: 'At least I'll have seen the coast of Greece.'

But as it turned out, she did more than that, for at the end of a boring day with no patients at all other than Mrs Bluett, now sitting in a chair and making a remarkable recovery. Octavia, having handed over to Mary, opened the hospital door leading to the foyer and found Doctor van der Weijnen waiting for her. He said without preamble: 'I have a car waiting, there's time enough to get you to the Acropolis, and we might even climb up to the Parthenon. Put on some flat shoes—you can have ten minutes.'

Octavia wasted a few precious seconds of those minutes gaping at him. Then: 'You're joking!'

He shook his head. 'No. I'll still be here when you come back in…' he glanced at his watch '…nine minutes.'

It was amazing what a girl could do in nine minutes, thought Octavia, thankful that she had the cabin to herself. She was out of her uniform, under the shower and into a sundress with its matching jacket within seven of those minutes. The remaining two she spent on her face and her hair with a second to spare for a quick spray of Madame Rochas. Her colour was a little heightened by the time she got back to the foyer, but otherwise she looked serene and cool. The doctor eyed her with appreciation. 'You're the only woman I've met who can dress in a hurry and look as though she has spent hours over it.'

A compliment which she recognised was of the highest order.

The next two hours were like an exciting dream; Octavia

was whisked on shore, thrust into a waiting car—a Citröen this time and as battered as the Fiat had been but more powerful—before she had collected her wits. They were through Piraeus and on the road to Athens, busy now with after-siesta traffic through which Lucas threaded his way, driving rapidly and without speaking, before she cried in an excited voice: 'Oh, look—there it is! The Acropolis, and that's the Parthenon on top of it…' She caught her breath. 'It's just as Father told me.'

Her companion took the car smartly between two overcrowded buses, to emerge calm and unscathed on the other side. 'A splendid sight, is it not? It can be seen from almost every point of the city. It is a pity that there isn't more time to see something of Athens, I'm afraid it's the Parthenon and nothing else.'

'You're awfully kind—I don't know how to thank you—I should never have had the chance…this is the second time…' She paused because it was difficult to put into words the fact that he had made it possible to go ashore twice already, but he didn't appear to notice her awkwardness, only remarked that it was possible to do quite a lot in two hours if one put one's mind to it.

'Well, yes,' she agreed, 'but only if there's a car waiting and someone to drive it who doesn't mind this traffic. You've been here before, of course.'

His 'yes' was brief. 'There is Hadrian's Gate on your right, but I don't dare to stop.'

They went on through the city and beyond to the foot of the Acropolis, where Octavia was urged to get out and put her best foot forward up the stony little path between the thickets and shrubs at its foot. It led them to a wider path, its stones worn slippery by countless feet and still crowded by sightseers going up and down it. The going got rougher as they climbed higher until the path petered out on to a rock-strewn area almost at the top, which still had to be climbed. Octavia, going as fast as she could from one steep step to the next, was glad of the doctor's hand holding hers and pulling her effortlessly from one to the other.

But at the top it was worth it. Octavia, ignoring the Parthenon for a moment, stopped to look at the view. 'It's like the Bible,' she observed, 'all those cypresses and those mountains and the little shrubs. Isn't it strange to think that all those centuries ago people stood here and admired the view?'

'And that in a thousand years or so someone else will be saying that about us. Shall we look around inside—there isn't a great deal of time.'

She followed him obediently as he led her round the magnificent ruin, not bothering her overmuch with a detailed history, merely outlining it and answering the questions with which she plied him.

'Built during the reign of Pericles, the latter half of the fifth century BC.' And when she remarked on its great columns: 'Marble, and no mortar.'

'Father told me to be sure and study the Propylaea and the Erechtheum with its caryatides.'

'My dear girl, we should need to spend a day here… the first is the entrance, and here is the Erechtheum. Take a quick look, because that's all the time we have.'

'At least I've seen them… Oh, I do thank you, Doctor van der Weijnen.'

'Lucas.' He was walking her briskly to a low wall. 'There—take a good look at that too, before we go back.'

Athens was spread out below them, its flat-roofed houses shimmering in the late afternoon sunshine. 'A pity we had no time to go to Delphi,' remarked Lucas. 'Next time, perhaps.'

'Oh, I don't suppose I'll come again, not for a long while, at any rate.'

'You will go back to St Maud's when we return to England?'

'I'm only filling a gap to oblige Mr Yates. He's the Senior Surgical Consultant…'

'We have met.' The doctor caught her arm and started back the way they had come, walking fast so that she had to skip and run a few steps to keep up. When they reached the little clearing where the guides sat, she tugged at his hand. 'Please—can we stop for just a moment so I can take one last look?'

He stopped at once and she turned to stare back up the hill at the lovely outline of the Parthenon. The doctor didn't look at all, he was staring in his turn at her face.

The traffic was worse on the way back and halfway there, waiting for a snarl-up of buses and donkey carts and cars to disentangle themselves, Octavia said apprehensively: 'They won't go without us, will they?'

His chuckle was reassuring. 'Unlikely—besides, there's still an hour before sailing time. Our shore leave expires in another fifteen minutes or so—there's plenty of time, so don't get all tensed up.'

'I am not all tensed up,' said Octavia a little edgily. 'I am a very calm and relaxed person.'

'So I have noticed. Ah, that bus is moving at last—we're off again.'

They got back with five minutes in hand, and on board once more she paused to thank him once again and was a little chilled by his formal politeness. She went below to the cabin and found it empty. She showered and dressed in blissful solitude, then went along to the library to change her book, where she met some of her table companions, who at once invited her to join them. And feeling as she did, for no reason that she knew of out of tune with her world, Octavia did so. But very shortly after dinner she excused herself on the plea of being on call that night, and went down to the cabin once more, where she wrote a long and somewhat muddled letter to her father and then went along to the hospital. Mary was still there, she supposed, for she had seen Sister Wise on deck after dinner.

'Has Joan Wise been on duty at all today?' she asked Mary as she slipped quietly into the duty room.

'No—she said she had a lot of time owing to her.' Mary grinned. 'I've never known such a muddle, but it'll be better tomorrow, though you're out of luck, Octavia, you're on duty from one o'clock until eight in the evening. She's on at eight in the morning until you take over. I suppose she's going ashore. I'm on call tomorrow night, but I'm free all day. So's Colin.'

'Good for you,' said Octavia, and meant it. 'What about the next day? Is that written in yet?'

'Yes. Alexandria. We dock about eight in the morning and leave at midnight. You're on duty again until four o'clock, then Joan takes over from you. You could get ashore for the evening if you had someone to go with.'

Octavia thought of Lucas and decided that it was unlikely that he would repeat his kindness for a third time. 'I don't much want to go ashore,' she remarked airily. 'What about you?'

'I'm on call for the night again. She's got it wrong, you know—you should be doing that and having a free day…'

'Oh, who cares?' Octavia smiled at her companion. 'How's Mrs Bluett?'

It was tantalising to have to watch everyone go ashore at Rhodes, but Octavia reminded herself that she had been very lucky so far. It was a glorious morning and she was free for an hour or two still, so she looked her fill at the harbour entrance guarded at either side by the statues of deer and at the town beyond, then went along for a swim in the deserted pool before going to an early lunch.

There had been no patients, Joan Wise told her coldly when she went on duty. Mrs Bluett was progressing just as she ought and there were a number of small chores which Octavia might do. She nodded briefly and went away without mentioning anything about the off-duty, and didn't bother to answer when Octavia politely wished her a pleasant afternoon. It was a pity that Joan Wise disliked her so much, she thought; the whole trip could have been the greatest fun if they had all got on well together. Octavia sighed gently and went along to see how Mrs Bluett did.

The afternoon passed slowly. Eight o'clock seemed a long way off and she couldn't help feeling that by the time that hour was reached, she wouldn't feel like doing much. Mary, bless her, had offered to relieve her an hour or two earlier, but Octavia had declined. It was hard enough on Mary having to get into uniform at eight o'clock in the evening anyway. She did the jobs Joan had listed, played a game of cards with Mrs Bluett, and after that lady's tea, tucked her up in bed again ready for her husband's visit. He had been ashore, so that the pair of them would have plenty to talk about.

It was almost seven o'clock when she heard the door open and looked up to see Lucas standing there. She had supposed him to be on shore, which now she came to think about it was nonsense, because Colin was free and one of them had to be on duty. She got to her feet and said: 'Good evening, Doctor van der Weijnen,' and then when he didn't speak, 'Mrs Bluett is very comfortable, her husband's with her—shall I ask him to wait for a few minutes?'

'Please—I won't be above a minute or two.'

They went together into the ward and afterwards the doctor went along to speak to Mr Bluett. Octavia went back into the duty room and shut the door, only to have it opened almost immediately.

'So you didn't see Rhodes,' remarked the doctor, shutting it again behind him.

'No. But I'm not here to see the sights, am I? I've been very lucky so far...'

He bent over and took the duty book from the desk and looked through it.

'You are on duty again at Alexandria.'

She hastened to make light of it. 'Not all the time—I can go ashore in the evening.'

He stared at her, frowning. 'I should hardly recommend you going ashore on your own—unless someone has offered to take you?'

'No, nobody has. Actually, I don't much want to go. Mary was telling me that it's not a bit glamorous, not in the city at any rate.'

'She's quite right.'

She turned in her chair to look up at him. 'Have you been there too? I didn't know you'd been on this ship before.'

'I haven't.' He was frowning again over the book in his hand. 'This off-duty seems to be remarkably muddled and most unfairly allocated.'

She looked away from his searching eyes. 'Oh, I expect it's a bit awkward to arrange.'

He tossed the book on to the desk. 'Perhaps. I should have enjoyed taking you around Rhodes, there are some charming villages.'

Octavia tried to think of something to say to that and came up with a mumbled, 'How kind.'

'You're off duty at eight o'clock?'

She nodded.

'So am I. Would you be too tired to dance for an hour or so?'

'Me? No, I'd like to very much.' She added: 'Am I allowed to? I mean, is it…?'

He laughed. 'If you mean will Joan Wise object, I can't see that that will matter in the least.' He opened the door, preparing to go. 'Wear that pink dress you had on the other evening, it suits you.'

They danced together for an hour or more and when half way through that time Octavia suggested that she intended to have an early night, he had said blandly: 'My dear Octavia, after such a sedentary day as yours has been, exercise is exactly what you need.'

So she had given up willingly enough and after that she had enjoyed herself. Like all large men, the doctor was a good dancer, and she was no mean performer herself. They waltzed and foxtrotted and tangoed and danced the bossa-nova until she at length declared she really would have to go to bed.

'A breath of fresh air,' suggested the doctor. 'Is this your wrap? You had better put it on.'

It was a clear night, the moon carving a golden path across the sea, the air pleasantly cool now. They walked up and down the deck, not saying much, and their long silences were companionable enough for Octavia to feel no need to break them; somehow they had passed the point where it was necessary to make conversation, although, she reflected, that was something they had never done. Considering how very little she knew about Lucas, she felt remarkably at ease with him.

When finally she declared that she would go to her cabin, he opened the heavy door to the foyer, only to let it close again, and when she looked at him in surprise he bent and kissed her, hard and swiftly. 'You shall go ashore at

Malta,' he promised her softly, and opened the door again and waited while she went past him.

Octavia had said nothing because she had been too surprised; his kiss had been quite unexpected and she had no idea how to behave. She gave him a small, shy smile and crossed the foyer and went down the staircase without looking at him again. By the time she reached the cabin, common sense had routed the medley of half-formed thoughts chasing round inside her head. She had been kissed before, dozens of times, and thought very little of it, but somehow this time it had seemed different; probably he had done it as a kind of seal on his promise that she should visit Malta.

The *Socrates* had sailed during the late afternoon and wouldn't arrive at Alexandria until mid-morning two days later, and the next day proved to be the busiest the surgery had experienced since the cruise had started. A number of the passengers had eaten unwisely and were keeping to their beds, and just for a few hours they had run into heavy weather so that there was a good deal of seasickness, severe enough to warrant the doctor's care. Besides these, several people had minor ills, so that the waiting room was crowded and Octavia, who wasn't due to go on duty until one o'clock, found herself in the surgery helping Colin, because Joan Wise, whose duty it was, was unable to deal with so many patients. But it was only temporary; by nightfall the weather had changed again to a calm sea and bright evening sunshine and everyone was looking forward to Alexandria, their small ailments forgotten.

There were only a handful left on board by noon on the following day and Octavia, watching Joan Wise and Mary going ashore, was glad that she had something to do. There was no one ill, even Mrs Bluett was nicely out of danger by now, but all the same, she would have to keep an eye on them all. She turned away from the rail and then paused. Lucas was going ashore, and there was another officer with him; she couldn't see who it was. They got into a car on the quay and drove away, and she watched it disappear round the corner of the passenger terminal and wished that she was in it too. But only for a moment. 'You're getting sorry for yourself, my girl,' she told herself. 'Remember you're here to work.'

The day passed more quickly than she had expected; she had some leisure too and spent it leaning over the rail watching the bustle on the quay—officials hurrying to and fro, men in long robes, their heads covered, standing silently, just looking around them. Octavia wondered if they had work or if they had just taken a few hours off to idle them away staring at the *Socrates*. There were men begging, too, and selling things—sunhats, jewellery, souvenirs; they saw her and she could hear them offering their wares even though she shook her head at them. There was a conjuror too, doing tricks with tiny chicks, making them disappear and reappear unendingly and looking up hopefully between each trick; in the end she threw him some small coins, anxious that he should stop so that the small creatures might have a few minutes' peace. A mistake, as everyone else had seen her gesture and came running, shouting their wares at the tops of their voices; there was nothing to do but to go below.

Joan Wise and Mary had shared a taxi to the Pyramids and wouldn't be back until later in the evening. Octavia ate her dinner with Colin, saw to her patients for the night and then went to sit in the duty room with a book. It had been a long day, but she hadn't minded, and there was Malta to look forward to. Lucas had said that she should go ashore and she had no reason to doubt him.

They were at sea all the next day and Octavia, on duty

at one o'clock again, had little to do, although the evening surgery kept her busy for an hour or so; a passenger with high blood pressure had lost her pills and needed to be examined before she could be prescribed more; a man on the kitchen staff had cut his finger badly and needed stitches and one of the crew had tripped over a ladder and lacerated his shins. Lucas took surgery, acknowledging her cheerful greeting with a rather austere nod and only speaking to her when it was necessary. His coolness annoyed her a little; surely he didn't suppose that she had taken his kiss seriously—after all, she wasn't a green girl. She finished her work, tidied up, asked him if he required her services further and when he said no without looking up from his writing, wished him goodbye in a severely professional voice.

She didn't see him for the rest of the evening, and even the news that she was free to go ashore at Malta on the following morning, if she wished, did little to please her. It didn't please Joan Wise either, she could see that, but she was due to have shore leave and even if Lucas hadn't promised it, she thought it likely that she would have had it anyway; Joan had done her best to cut her off-duty, but even she couldn't go too far. Octavia went to bed in a peevish frame of mind and went on duty at eight o'clock quite wishing that something drastic might happen so that she was prevented from visiting Malta at all.

But nothing did, and when she saw the island ahead of her and the *Socrates* slid slowly into the harbour's narrow mouth, she was glad of it. It was magnificent; Valetta, rising straight from the rocky shore, seemed to be part of those same rocks. There were houses within a few feet of the water giving way presently to a small quay, from which a road led uphill to the town and in the distance the shipyards on the other side of the Grand Harbour. Octavia hung over the rail with everyone else, watching the great ship being manoeuvred to its anchorage. They would have to go ashore in the launches and passengers were already making their way to the gangways. She hoped that it wouldn't take too long; they were to sail again by four o'clock. Luckily surgery had been small that morning and although it was barely ten o'clock she had already changed into a cotton dress, handed over to Mary and was ready to go ashore at the earliest moment.

The launches filled and began their ferrying to and fro. Another half an hour, she calculated, and she would be able to go too—in the meantime there was plenty to see. The passengers thinned at last and Octavia decided to go down to where the launches waited. She paused to take a final look as she left the rail and then looked again; Doctor van der Weijnen was going ashore, she could see his huge frame standing by one of the junior officers in charge of the launch. So he hadn't meant a word he had said. All the same, she would go ashore and see as much as she could in the time she had. She had money enough to get a taxi and she knew where she wanted to go.

Everyone was very cheerful during the short trip ashore and several of her companions invited her to join them, but she refused nicely because she suspected that most of them already knew the island and wouldn't want to re-visit the places she had set her heart on seeing. She was one of the last to leave the launch and walked slowly across the quay to the street which would take her to the town above; probably there would be a taxi, if not she would walk the short distance and find one there. She went round the side of the small Customs building and looked around her. The last of the buses with the passengers had gone on their various tours, the street was more or less empty, but not quite. Doctor van de Weijnen was leaning up against a wall watching her from the opposite pavement.

As soon as she saw him he crossed the street to her. 'I came on ahead,' he told her briskly, 'to see about hiring a car. It's this Austin.' He held the door open for her to get in and when she didn't: 'Is anything the matter?'

She looked up at him with her beautiful eyes and said seriously: 'No—not now. I thought you'd forgotten. I saw you in the launch…' She still made no attempt to move. 'You're sure you want to…?'

'I am astonished that a beautiful girl like you should doubt even for one moment that anyone could do less than leap at a chance to spend an hour or two in your company.'

Her mouth curved into a wide smile. 'What a flowery speech!'

He laughed. 'Wasn't it? I practised it for hours just in case you got uppity.'

She laughed with him and got into the car. 'I suppose you've been here before, too?' she asked him.

'Yes. I had an aunt—dead now—who was married to someone who lived in Mdina. I used to come here when I was a boy, soon after the war ended.'

They had climbed the hill to the town and had reached the square, full of parked buses, and Lucas parked the car. 'No cars inside the walls,' he explained, 'we go through this gate.'

He didn't hurry her but allowed her to stop and peer down narrow side streets, crane her neck to see the buildings around them and pause at one or other of the small shops until presently they came to the market square in front of the Cathedral of St John. It was busy and bright and the noise was intense as they made their way to the cathedral steps. At the top Octavia fished a scarf out of a pocket and draped it over her hair and Lucas said approvingly: 'Good—you're such a sensible girl. Sleeves too—so many women forget.' A remark which gave her only tepid pleasure, although probably he had meant it as a compliment.

The cathedral was magnificent. They wandered round the chapels and inspected the tombs of the Knights of St John and then wandered out again to visit the Triton Fountain and have coffee at the Phoenicia Hotel before getting in the car and driving the short journey to Mdina. They left the car outside the great gate once more and walked through the little town, quiet and peaceful and old, its great houses shuttered against the bright sun, and then spent half an hour in a shop selling local handiwork where Octavia, quite carried away, bought a shawl, lace and some silver filigree work and a beautifully knitted cardigan. The doctor, who had remained quietly beside her while she made her purchases, only spoke when she held this garment up for his inspection. 'Very nice,' he commented, 'but surely a little on the large side for you?'

'It's not for me—it's for Mrs Lovelace, she's Father's daily housekeeper, and she likes blue.'

He carried the parcels without complaint and led her back through the narrow street to a small restaurant and bar where they had their lunch and Octavia sampled *timpana*, a pie of macaroni and minced meat, and washed it down with dark, rich coffee. They had to leave soon after that, going back the way they had come because there wasn't much time. It was as they were entering Valetta again that Lucas remarked: 'It is a great pity that you were unable to see Rhodes; the Street of the Knights and the Palace and all the delightful villages away from the town…'

'Well, yes—I was disappointed. But I have seen Malta,

haven't I? or some of it at any rate. You've been very kind…'

He didn't answer her but took the Austin down the hill to the landing stage and helped her out. There were only a few people waiting for the launches, most of them had already returned, and ten minutes later they were on board again. They went along the deck together and then went through to one of the foyers and started down the stairs.

'Well, I suppose I must take over from Colin,' said the doctor. 'And you, Octavia?'

'I'm on duty,' she told him.

'Then we shall be seeing each other again.' He nodded briefly, listened silently to her thanks, smiled faintly and went away.

And certainly they saw each other again, but now he was the doctor and she the nurse, for there was a sudden spate of trivial hurts and cuts which kept them busy until early evening. Presently Lucas went away, leaving her to finish her duty on her own. She saw to Mrs Bluett, got the surgery ready for the morning and then sat thinking about her day. It had been delightful and she had enjoyed it, and what was more she had enjoyed Lucas's company. Rather more than was good for her peace of mind.

CHAPTER FIVE

THE Hampshire coast looked green and peaceful even though there was a fine drizzle. Octavia took a peep at it out of the surgery porthole while Colin examined a sprained ankle, surprised to find that there was a sense of relief in seeing it again as well as regret. She could think of no good reason for these feelings; the remaining days of the cruise had been pleasant enough and Joan Wise had—surprisingly—been meticulous about sharing the off-duty fairly between the three of them. Whether it was coincidence or clever contriving on her part, Octavia couldn't be sure, but somehow Octavia's duty had coincided with Colin and never with Professor van der Weijnen, and since he had made no attempt to seek her out when she was free, she had taken great care to avoid him. It had meant turning tail and going the other way when she caught sight of him at the end of a deck or mounting a staircase she was about to go down, but she had felt reasonably sure that he hadn't seen her, and on a ship as vast as the *Socrates*, it hadn't been too difficult.

She turned away from her contemplation of the coastline, very near now, and handed Colin the strapping, agreeing with genuine sympathy that it was very hard luck that their patient, Mrs Drew, should be forced to hobble down the gangway at the end of what should have been a perfect holiday.

'Though I've enjoyed myself,' said that lady cheerfully, 'and it was my fault for wearing those high heels. Tom said I ought to have changed them and I wouldn't listen.' She beamed up at Octavia. 'You see, love, I'm fat, which does make it awkward. Do you two get a holiday now?'

'I don't,' Colin told her. 'Nurse Lock doesn't either; she's going back to her hospital.'

Mrs Drew tutted sympathetically. 'Well, I never did, after all your hard work, too. And that other nice doctor, the one with the foreign accent—doesn't he get a holiday either?'

'I don't imagine so. The regular ship's doctor should be back for the next cruise to the Caribbean.'

'So the poor man will be out of work,' declared Mrs Drew with instant concern.

'Well, no, I don't imagine so; he's quite well established as a doctor.'

He straightened up. 'How does that feel, Mrs Drew? We'll let you have a stick—you'll need some kind of support.'

'Thank you, dear. You've both been very kind. Now I'm going to put the last few things in the overnight bag. We're almost there, aren't we?'

'Another hour or so.'

'A nice crowd on this trip,' remarked Colin when he had closed the door upon Mrs Drew. 'Have you enjoyed it, Octavia? Can't say I take much notice of these things, but it seemed to me that you had more than your fair share of duty.'

'Well, I'm only filling in, after all,' she conceded. 'Won't you and Mary get any time together before the ship sails this evening?'

He grinned. 'You bet we will! We're due a couple of weeks' leave when we get back from it, we're going to get engaged—I daresay you guessed.'

Octavia smiled. 'Well, yes, I think I did. I hope you'll both be very happy. Are you going to stay with the ship?'

He shook his head. 'No—another three months perhaps and then I'll try for a junior partnership and we can get married.' He got up and stretched. 'If that's the lot, we could start closing down.'

It didn't take long. They checked the drugs together, and Octavia whisked round the surgery, returning it to its pristine state; the wards had been dealt with on the previous day, for Mrs Bluett was back in her cabin now and would leave the ship first to be transported to hospital for a check-up before going home.

'There's the pilot coming on board,' said Colin suddenly. 'We're almost home.'

He went away presently and Octavia went in her turn, finished packing her overnight bag and put everything ready to change. She was on duty until the last of the passengers had disembarked, but it was still well before noon, so she should be home by teatime. She fetched a sigh for no reason at all and went on deck to look around.

Most of the passengers were ready to leave the ship even though it would be another hour or so before they could do so. The decks were almost deserted and although the fine rain had stopped by now the day was dull and a little chilly, she shivered in her thin uniform and went down to the library, where she leafed through the books on the shelves and then, tired of that, went to see how much longer it would be before they docked.

The *Socrates* was sidling gently up against the dock, inching her way delicately like a lady in slippers going carefully through mud. Finally she stopped, so soundlessly that Octavia was hardly aware of it, only the sight of the gangways being run out confirmed it. It was quite some time before the first of the passengers, led by Mrs Bluett in a wheelchair and escorted by Joan Wise as far as the ambulance, began to leave the ship in a steady and increasingly larger trickle. Octavia craned her neck to see the last of her patient and then turned her attention to the orderly stream of people leaving the ship. She would be going herself soon, there was nothing left for her to do; she had been paid, made her farewells to everyone she had had anything to do with on board, there was only the last-minute change from uniform to her coffee-coloured outfit with the addition this time of a light camel coat. Indeed, she might have done that half an hour ago, but she had delayed it, not admitting to herself that her reason for doing so was because she hadn't seen Lucas. She had been avoiding him, but that was no reason for not wishing him goodbye. But there had been no sign of him, and nothing, she told herself stoutly, would induce her to go in search of him.

There was no need. His voice, calm and matter-of-fact behind her, made her jump.

'I'll drive you home, Octavia.'

She knew that there was nothing she would have liked better, all the same she said instantly in a tart voice: 'You made me jump! Thank you for the offer, but I've already made arrangements.'

'Cancel them.'

She turned to look at him. 'And supposing I don't want to?' she enquired with deceptive mildness.

His mildness more than equalled hers. 'I hope you will change your mind; I should like to talk to you.'

'What about?' She had turned away from him and was giving an answering wave to a passenger going ashore.

'Will you marry me, Octavia?'

She whipped round to stare at him blankly, her pretty mouth half open. He looked as he always did, calm, faintly arrogant and showing no flattering eagerness for her answer. She closed her mouth with something of a snap and then opened it to say: 'Why should you want to marry me?' and added, 'I'm surprised.'

'That is to be expected. I am aware that I have given you little indication of my intentions.' He fell silent for a moment. 'I believe that we would suit each other very well. You are a handsome young woman, you are calm, resourceful, efficient and a pleasant companion—and that is all I want, Octavia. I can't pretend affection—love, although I like you enormously.'

She found her voice, and was surprised when it emerged quite steady and as calm as his. 'I can't think why you should want to marry me, though; your reasons aren't very good.'

'I have told you I am a widower; have been for eight years. I'm thirty-nine—I have a daughter, nine years old, and we both need someone.'

'Surely you have a housekeeper, or a governess or—or something?' She gave him a thoughtful look. 'What you really need is a good housekeeper.'

'No,' he told her blandly, 'if I had wanted a housekeeper, I should have found one, and as it happens, I have already—Juffrouw Hinksma has been with me for a long time now.'

She couldn't resist remarking: 'She must be a paragon!'

'She is. You haven't answered my question.'

'You don't really expect me to? You can't be serious?'

'I am.' He smiled at her with such charm that she quite forgot that she believed him to be joking. 'But don't answer now, for you will say no, won't you? Let me drive you home while you think it over.'

'But I know now; I don't need to think it over—there's absolutely no point in waiting to tell you.'

Now his smile was as bland as his voice had been, scything through her common sense. 'But wait all the same, Octavia. It's not impossible, you know. Oh, we fall out, you and I, but you must have noticed that we enjoy each other's company too.' He sighed. 'I've been lonely—I didn't realise that, and I daresay Berendina has been lonely too. I've met girls I have liked, but never one I could have married—indeed, I had not thought of marrying again, but now I've changed my mind. And you fit all my requirements; you will make an excellent doctor's wife, understanding and accepting late hours and interrupted meals, disorganised days and changed plans and lending a hand when it is necessary.'

'No,' said Octavia, quite positively, 'I'm quite sure...'

He continued just as though she hadn't spoken. 'I live in den Haag, quite a pleasant house, and I have a number of friends there—some of them are English. Berendina goes to day school; you would have plenty of freedom.'

She thought with sudden anger that it wasn't freedom she wanted; love and companionship and laughter together and children, those were the things she wanted. 'I'm sorry,' she told him, 'I can't even consider it.'

'You are already engaged, perhaps?' His voice was remarkably placid.

'No, nothing like that. I have my father to think of; I see him very frequently now; he isn't so very old, but he's forgetful and rather—well, unworldly. I don't think I could go away and leave him.'

'There are ways...' Lucas paused and then went on

smoothly: 'Well, at least allow me to drive you home. We won't discuss it any more if you don't wish to.'

It would have been churlish to have refused. Besides, now she thought about it she would be sorry not to see him again; perhaps in other circumstances and if they had got to know each other well, she might have—well, not have found it so very surprising.

'In about an hour, then. I'll be in the main foyer—have you much luggage?'

'A case and an overnight bag. Is your car here?'

'Yes—I brought it over several days before I came on board. I come to England fairly often.'

It was on the tip of her tongue to ask him why, but she thought better of it. He would think her merely curious, and she had no right to be that.

He was waiting for her when she reached the foyer an hour later. He took her luggage from the cabin steward, beckoned a porter, and followed her down the gangway. On the quay, she paused a moment and looked up at the mighty ship. 'Well, that was an experience,' she observed, 'and I've seen quite a lot of the world.'

He smiled at her. 'Perhaps it would have been more enjoyable without the—er—encumbrances of work.'

The Customs shed was almost empty by now. They were delayed for only a few minutes before they emerged at its other end, now almost free of cars, and these few dominated by a sleek dark blue Rolls-Royce convertible. Octavia gave it an admiring glance and scanned the assortment of Austins, Triumphs, Citröens and Fiats, wondering which would belong to the doctor.

None of them. He stopped at the Rolls, opened its door and invited her to get in. 'Oh, my!' exclaimed Octavia. 'It's not yours, is it?'

'Er—yes. I need a reliable car.' He got in beside her. 'And a roomy one, too.'

True enough, she thought, he seemed to take up a good deal of space, but surely there were other cars, not as wildly expensive as a Rolls, which would have been large enough to accommodate his vast frame? She said, 'Yes, of course,' because she couldn't think of anything better to say, and lapsed into silence.

There was a lot of traffic in the city, but Lucas sliced neatly through it, taking every advantage of the car's unobtrusive power, to join the Winchester road presently. Here he could travel faster; he overtook everything ahead of him and covered the ten miles or so to the Winchester bypass in no time at all. Just before they reached it Octavia asked: 'Do you know which way to go?'

He steadied the Rolls's silent rush as they reached the bypass. 'Yes—but you'll have to direct me when we reach Alresford.' He glanced at her. 'And now tell me, what did you think of being a ship's nurse?'

'Fun,' she said instantly, 'provided everyone gets on with everyone else. Only not quite busy enough for me, I think. I'm used to people pouring in round the clock, you see, and I felt guilty when I didn't have anything to do.'

'Me too,' he commented surprisingly. 'I wonder why our Miss Wise had her knife so firmly in you?' He chuckled. 'No, don't answer that! You're young and very pretty and a first class nurse, and she is not so young and perhaps getting a little out of date with her work.'

'We can't all like each other,' said Octavia stiffly.

He edged past a car load of people trailing a caravan. 'And what a good thing that is,' he said cheerfully. 'All the same, she could have been a little more forthcoming with your duty hours. Of all the muddles!'

'Oh, you thought so too? But you see, if one isn't in

the constant habit of working out the off-duty, it's—it's difficult.'

'Rubbish. Three of you and twenty-four hours in the day—nothing could have been easier. I told her so.'

'Oh—did she mind?'

She didn't see his grin. 'I wrapped it up very neatly. She was convinced that you deserved shore leave at Sicily and that she had meant you to have it all the time.'

'Oh, so it was you...?'

'Well, I was the boss,' he murmured apologetically. 'But I had to put my foot down hard at Malta.'

They were climbing towards the roundabout which would lead them to the Alresford road and there weren't many more miles to go. 'You were very kind,' said Octavia, and longed to ask him why he had done it.

He answered her unspoken question for her. 'You had mentioned that your father had given you a list of the splendours you should see; it seemed a pity that you should have to return without having seen one of them.'

For some reason she felt disappointed, and that wasn't the only reason, either. He had said that he wouldn't discuss his extraordinary proposal, but she had quite thought that he would; perhaps he hadn't meant a word of it, although it really didn't matter; she had no intention of accepting. She was quite content with her life, she told herself firmly; there was John Waring, and she had her father to think of. She ignored the fact that she had no intention of marrying John; he had been unpleasantly possessive and ill-tempered when she had told him about her temporary job, and as for her father, she had to admit that although they loved each other dearly, there was nothing she could do to make his life happier. Indeed, if she were to return home and live there he wouldn't care for it; Mrs Lovelace was used to his absentmindedness about meals and appointments and allowed him to be comfortable without fussing about spoiled food and piles of dusty papers. Whereas she herself would probably drive him mad within a few weeks. She smiled at the thought of her elderly, much loved parent and Lucas asked:

'Glad to be home again? Where do I go from here?'

She directed him up the main street and told him to turn left at its top and then left again, away from the bustling shops lining the wide shopping centre, and then directed him to stop before her home.

'You'll come in and meet Father?' she asked, and knocked on the door. There was no reply, so she turned the handle and went down the passage, calling to her father as she went. Mrs Lovelace would be out shopping probably, but it surprised her that her father didn't answer, but perhaps he was so wrapped up in something or other that he just hadn't heard. She called over her shoulder: 'Do come in—Father will be in his study…'

She opened a door as she spoke and paused to glance round the untidy booklined room. She saw her father sitting in his chair by the small fire, but he didn't turn his head as she crossed the room to him, so that she exclaimed half laughing: 'Father…' and then more urgently: 'Father?'

She saw him smile then and heard his faint: 'Octavia—I wanted to see you again,' before his head dropped sideways against the chair.

She didn't realise that she had called Lucas by name, only that he was there beside her, bending over her father and then gently walking her to a chair and sitting her down. He said in a voice as gentle as his manner: 'Your father is dead, Octavia.'

She said wildly: 'He can't be—he spoke, he looked at me. You must do something!' She heard her voice crack and made herself stop.

Lucas had gone back to the still figure in the chair, but presently he straightened himself and came back to her, standing in front of her so that she could see nothing. 'I'm sorry, Octavia, if there was anything to be done I would have done it. Be happy that by God's good grace he did see you and speak to you and died without knowing it. No, don't get up. Where do you keep the brandy?'

'I don't want...' she began, and then said obediently: 'It's in the cupboard over there,' and waited while he fetched a glass and put it into her hand.

'Drink that and tell me the name of your father's doctor—I'll telephone him.'

The spirit took her breath, but it made her feel as though she were a person again and not just someone in a dream. She gave name and telephone number in a controlled little voice and drank the rest of the brandy, dimly aware that Lucas was telephoning. After that the next hour or so was a blur in which Doctor Dodds came and went again, and during that time he had talked to her, although she had no idea what he had said. She remembered Lucas asking her to go to the kitchen and make coffee. She hadn't wanted to go; to make coffee at such a time seemed an uncaring thing to do. It wasn't until she came back presently with the tray that she discovered that while she had been in the kitchen, her father had been taken upstairs to his own room. She had drunk some of hers, doing as Lucas told her like an obedient child, not listening to the two men talking together and not wanting to know what they were saying. She felt numb. Nothing of the nightmare was true; presently she would wake up and discover that her father was there, in his chair, immersed in some book. Doctor Dodds had shaken her by the hand and smiled very kindly at her and told her to leave everything to Doctor van der Weijnen, something she didn't quite take in, for when the older man had gone she asked in a wooden voice: 'Will you tell me what I have to do? Mrs Lovelace will be back shortly, I should think…I have to have a certificate, don't I? And take it to…and see about the…' She paused to swallow back the great lump in her throat. 'You've been very kind. I'm sorry I can't offer you lunch before you go.'

He pulled up a chair and sat astride it, his arms resting on its back, watching her. He said in a voice kind enough to melt the lump: 'You'll stay just where you are, I'll attend to everything.'

She stared at him. 'But you'll want to get back…'

'No, there is no hurry about that. I shall stay here. Tell me which room I can use and I'll bring in our luggage and as soon as Mrs Lovelace returns I'll get things started.'

And he did just that, coping with the housekeeper when she returned, persuading her to pull herself together and get a meal of sorts for all of them, and doing it so well that Mrs Lovelace tossed down the brandy he offered her and declared herself ready to do anything she could to help Miss Octavia. 'For a nicer young lady I've yet to meet,' she told him, 'and that thoughtful for her pa—coming home as often as she could to be with him when she could have been having a good time in London.' She eyed the doctor thoughtfully. 'And you, sir, if I might be so bold as to ask? Are you staying? Who's to see to all that's necessary?'

'Yes, I'm staying, Mrs Lovelace, and I'll attend to everything, although I should be grateful for some information—I don't want to worry Octavia.'

They sat down to lunch presently and Octavia pushed the food round and round her plate and made no attempt to answer her companion's quiet flow of talk; it served as a background to her thoughts which were chaotic.

Lucas's quiet: 'I should have liked to have known your

father, Octavia,' cut through them like a knife and she looked up from her plate to exclaim:

'Oh, I can't believe it, he was only sixty-seven. I know he was absentminded, but he was always so well.'

She got up from the table and Lucas got up with her. 'Oh, what am I to do?' she cried, and burst into the comfort of tears at last.

'We'll discuss that later.' Lucas spoke softly and she barely heard him, but his arms round her shoulders were comforting and solid and he held her fast while she sobbed her heart out against his jacket. Presently she gave a prodigious sniff and lifted a blotched, puffy-eyed face to his.

'So sorry—men hate women crying, don't they? But I—I just couldn't help it.'

'I should have found you very extraordinary if you hadn't, Octavia.' He took a handkerchief from his pocket and wiped her wet face in a matter-of-fact fashion which she found very soothing. 'And now we're going to sit down while I tell you what has been arranged.'

He did so, quietly and with a calmness which steadied her nerves nicely, and when he had finished she was able to give him a list of people who would like to come to the funeral and even discuss its time and date.

'Good, that's clear enough. I'll do some more telephoning if I may and then you shall take me round the town. It looked delightful as we came through it.'

It didn't matter what she did, she might as well walk as stay in the house, she supposed, and he was being kind. She sat quietly while he telephoned, not really listening until she became aware that he was speaking his own language, and when he had finished: 'I had to let someone know at home—I hope you don't mind?'

'No, of course not. I—I'm putting you to a great deal of trouble.'

His 'No,' was so decisive that she didn't say any more but got to her feet and accompanied him out of the house. They walked a long way and his continuous flow of undemanding conversation prevented her from thinking her own thoughts. She was tired by the time they got back to the house, to find Mrs Lovelace waiting with the tea tray. And after tea Octavia went to sleep, curled up in one of the shabby armchairs in the sitting room, and Lucas, who had been sitting some way away from her, came and sat close beside her so that when she woke after half an hour or so it was his face she saw when she opened her eyes, and his hand which took hers as she jerked upright.

'Waking up is the worst part, isn't it?' He smiled at her. 'Believe me, it won't be as bad as this for long—time really does heal.'

'You know about it, don't you?' Of course he did, she reminded herself; he had lost his wife.

'My mother died last year.'

'I'm sorry.' She added impulsively: 'I hope there was someone to be kind to you just as you're being kind to me.' Just for a moment she wanted to cry again, but she managed not to. 'You're sure you don't mind staying? What time do you want to go tomorrow?'

'I'm not going tomorrow. I shall stay until after the funeral. We can be married the following day, very quietly, and go back to Holland together.'

Octavia listened to this astonishing speech with her mouth open. 'Marry you? But I never said…I don't think I…'

'My dear, does it not seem a most sensible thing to do? You no longer have your father to think of. Where would you go? Back to St Maud's? And keep this house? How would you manage that? Get a post locally, perhaps—but I imagine a place this size has either no hospital at all or a very small one—you would be bored stiff. Forgive me, but will the house be yours?'

She nodded. 'Yes, but Father—Father said that he hadn't much money—I don't suppose I could afford to keep it going. I'll have to sell it.'

'Supposing we think about that later. There would be no hurry; you could think about it and decide what you wish to do. I am aware that I'm not being quite fair discussing marriage with you at such a time, but on the other hand to wait seems needlessly wasteful of time. All that I have said holds good; it is only for you to decide.'

'But I don't love you,' said Octavia. 'At least, I like you very much and I daresay we would get on quite well—besides, I shall be a perfect misery for a little while.' She managed a crooked little smile. 'So I don't think...'

'We discussed the question of not loving, did we not? I haven't changed my opinion and I don't suppose you have either. I think that we are well suited; your father's death has made no difference, Octavia, only to expedite our wedding. I'll get a special licence and make the arrangements. I think your father would have liked us to marry.' He stared at her hard. 'He would want to know that you had someone to look after you.'

She should have been able to argue with him, but it hardly seemed worthwhile; she really didn't care what happened to her, although the idea of going back to St Maud's made her unhappy and almost certainly she wouldn't be able to live in Alresford. Besides, even if there was enough money, what would she do with herself? Wither into an old maid? She sighed and said with a reluctance which brought a faint smile to her companion's mouth: 'Do you really think it would work? Supposing it turns out to be a mistake?'

'It won't.' He sounded so cheerful about it that she found

herself believing him, all the same she left no stone of doubt unturned. 'Berendina—just supposing she hates the sight of me?'

Lucas had gone to stand by the window. 'She won't,' he assured her easily. 'I know my daughter—only a week or so ago she was begging me to find her a mama, someone pretty and young and not severe. The child had a rather fiery governess for several years and now, even though she is very happy at school, she wants a mother like all the other children there.'

'Does she remember her mother?'

'She died when Berendina was one year old.' Something in his voice stopped her from asking any more questions and he went on: 'So you see, Octavia, we need you and you need us. Between us we can be a family instead of three lonely people.'

She knew in her heart that she had already given in, but something prompted her to ask: 'Wouldn't it be better if I just came on a visit—just to make sure?'

He was looking out of the window, but he glanced at her over his shoulder, smiling. 'I had thought of that, too.' He sounded reasonable and utterly dependable. 'But would it not be better for Berendina if you arrived, as it were, a ready-made mum? Besides, getting married in Holland involves a good deal more officialdom than it does here.' He added casually: 'Shall I see about a licence and if you don't feel up to it, we'll postpone it for the time being.'

'Well, yes—you're sure you don't mind doing that? I'm sorry to be so uncertain, but I—...it's all been rather unexpected.' Her voice trembled and she took a deep breath. 'You're being very kind.'

It seemed inadequate and she had said that before, but her brain wasn't working as well as it should. Perhaps, she thought tiredly, everything would be all right; Lucas was a kind man and she liked him. That he had a temper and could be arrogant she already knew, but she thought that he was, on the whole, a mild man, only roused to strong feelings when the occasion demanded them. She said hesitatingly: 'I'll marry you, Lucas—here before we go to Holland if you think that's best. I'll try and be a good wife to you, if—if you'll be patient.' She added: 'Father would have liked you.'

He crossed the room and pulled her gently out of her chair and stood with his hands on her shoulders, looking down at her. 'Thank you, my dear—that was one of the nicest things you have ever said to me. I don't think you will regret our marriage.' He bent and kissed her gently on her cheek and went on: 'And now we are going to have a drink and see what Mrs Lovelace has for our dinner, then you are going early to bed.'

'I shan't sleep.'

'Yes, you will, for I shall give you something to take care of that.'

The evening which Octavia had dreaded passed tolerably well; Lucas, surprisingly helpful, helped with their meal and washed the dishes afterwards, made coffee and then presently sent her up to bed, to appear shortly afterwards with the promised pill. Octavia, contrary to all her fears, slept all night.

CHAPTER SIX

OCTAVIA, thinking about it much later on, knew that she would never have got through the next few days if Lucas hadn't been there. He seemed to know exactly what to do and how and when to do it with the least possible fuss, attending to the sad details without bothering her at all and spending long hours driving her round the countryside or walking her relentlessly so that home, when they returned, wasn't a house of shadows but a haven for eating and sleeping. And he did all this with a calm friendliness and a solid sympathy which did much to ease her grief, talking, when she felt like it, of his home and work in a rather vague fashion which had left her with the impression of a fair-sized practice, a pleasant home and enough money to live on.

Perhaps, if she hadn't been so engrossed in her own thoughts, she might have wondered how he could afford to run a Rolls-Royce: as it was she barely gave it a thought, accepting her unexpected future with a docile mind. Lucas was a good man, she knew that, and even though there was no love between them, there was a strong liking. Whenever she thought of that future it was with a sense of relief that he would be in it, too.

And once the funeral was over there was no time to think too much about the time ahead. Lucas had driven up to London and arranged everything at the hospital without telling her too much about it: she had accepted the fact that it had been dealt with, just as she had accepted his practical arrangements concerning the house. For the time being it was to remain empty; they would return in a month or so when they could decide what was best to be done about it. There had been very little money, barely enough to pay for the expenses of the house for the next year and settle her father's small debts, but money hadn't seemed important.

She packed the best of her clothes, washed her hair and went early to bed at Lucas's suggestion. They were to be married in the morning and travel straight to Holland; an early night seemed sensible. Octavia was almost asleep when she remembered something. She jumped out of bed, pulled on her old dressing gown, because her best one was packed, and ran downstairs. Lucas was in the sitting room, sitting at the table, writing, and she thought fleetingly and with gratitude that it was just like him not to use her father's study. 'I've forgotten something,' she told him as he got to his feet. 'Mrs Lovelace—Father didn't leave her anything, and he would have, if he'd known…I'm not sure just how much money there is, but she must have something.'

Lucas walked round the table to stand before her. Her face, unmade-up and pale with sorrow, was still utterly charming, her hair hung loose round her shoulders and the elderly shapeless dressing gown quite failed to conceal her splendid shape. He gave her a quick glance and then looked sideways at the papers on the table. 'Of course Mrs Lovelace shall have something,' he assured her in an easy voice. 'In fact, I've just been going through these papers—there's enough to give her a cheque for five hundred pounds,' and at her surprised look, 'Oh, I know there's almost no ready money, but it can be drawn against the value of this house.'

'Oh, can it?' she asked uncertainly. 'I don't know much about such things, but if you say so…'

He gave a small reassuring nod. 'I'll see to it before I come to bed—you can give it to her before we go.' He smiled his kind smile. 'Go back to bed, Octavia, and go to sleep—I shall look in on you presently and if you're not I shall give you a sleeping pill.'

She was asleep within ten minutes; sorrow, she had discovered, was so much easier to bear when it was shared with someone who understood. As for the doctor, he sat down again, put aside the notes for a lecture he was preparing for the following week, and wrote out a cheque for five hundred pounds on his account at an English bank.

The morning was fine but chilly with a taste of autumn in the air. Octavia, wearing a grey flannel suit which was still fairly new, her best brown calf shoes and with her face nicely made up, got breakfast for them both, dried the dishes while Lucas washed them, and then, a pretty little hat in stitched silk on her head and her newest gloves on her hands, accompanied Lucas out to the car. It was only a few minutes' drive. She sat quietly beside him, not thinking about anything much, watching his well-kept hands on the wheel, noting the elegance of his dark grey suit and the perfection of the shoes on his very large feet. And he didn't disturb her vague thoughts. Only when they arrived at the church he opened the glove compartment and took out a small spray of pale pink roses and pinned them to her jacket. He thrust a white carnation into his own buttonhole too, smiled at her with such charm that she smiled back, suddenly much happier, and leaned across to open her door. 'Stay there,' he told her, and got out and came round to help her out too, then took her arm as they went into the quiet church.

Mrs Lovelace, the solicitor, Mr Pimm, and the vicar were already there; they all turned to smile as they walked towards them and Mrs Lovelace, who was of a romantic turn of mind and enjoyed a wedding even when there was no white satin and veil, wiped away a tear or two. The ceremony was brief and there was no one else there at all, because that was how Octavia had wanted it. Getting back into the car, Lucas's plain gold wedding ring on her finger, she had the feeling that none of it had really happened. Weddings were usually well-planned, elaborate functions with all one's friends and family, new clothes, smart hats, bridesmaids, a big bouquet...and yet, she reminded herself soberly, the words of the marriage service had been the same. She smiled a little shyly at Lucas, who smiled back at her with a cheerful: 'Hullo, Mevrouw van der Weijnen,' and her smile widened at that.

'Oh, yes of course!'

They went back to the house, where the vicar and Mr Pimm and Mrs Lovelace joined them and they all drank champagne before Octavia drew the housekeeper aside and gave her an envelope containing the cheque. And after that the luggage was stowed away in the Rolls' roomy boot and she got in beside Lucas again and was driven away while their three guests waved and called good luck. She turned round to get a last glimpse of the house but they were already turning the corner. If she had been alone, she had no doubt at all that she would have gone round her home, remembering the happy times she had spent in it and the unhappiness of the last few days, and probably crying a great deal too, but Lucas had given her no chance to do that; she had been whisked away almost before she had had time to realise it.

'We'll be coming back quite soon,' said Lucas's calm voice. 'You don't have to say goodbye.'

They had plenty of time; they were to sail from Harwich on the night boat and it was still barely eleven o'clock. 'We've so much time,' observed Lucas cheerfully, 'I thought we might turn off at Guildford and go across to Windsor. There's a rather nice Italian restaurant there with a splendid view of the castle, we could lunch and then make our way to Hemel Hempstead and Hertford and then cross country to Bishops Stortford, pick up the Braintree road and take the Colchester road from there; we can dine in a village close by—Dedham, at a delightful Flemish weaver's cottage turned restaurant, it's on the river bank and very peaceful.'

Octavia murmured, 'It sounds nice,' her thoughts still with her home and the life she had left behind her, but if Lucas noticed her aberration he chose to ignore it, continuing to talk about every subject under the sun excepting their marriage that morning, until presently he said gently: 'Why not talk about it, Octavia?'

She stirred in the well-upholstered leather seat. 'I don't know how to start.'

'Tell me about your mother. Are you like her?'

'Yes, only I'm a good deal bigger.'

'Then she must have been a beautiful woman—how did she and your father meet?'

It was easier after that. Octavia, lost in a world of reminiscence, hardly noticed the scenery, and it was the greatest surprise to her when Lucas slowed the car as they entered Windsor. 'Oh, lord, I must have been boring you,' she exclaimed contritely. 'I had no idea…'

'I haven't been bored.' He sounded friendly and relaxed, 'and you feel better for it, don't you?'

'Yes. It—it was as good as a good howl.'

He threaded the car through the traffic into Thames Street. 'Better—but if you feel like a good howl at any time, don't hesitate. Grief can't be ignored, but it can be softened. I can promise you, my dear, that it will be more bearable each day that passes.' Just for a moment his hand closed over hers, and then: 'Here we are. Have you ever eaten saltimbocca? Because now is your chance to do so.'

And in the face of his calm matter-of-fact kindness, she ate. What was more, she ate with the beginnings of her usual healthy appetite.

They sat over their meal and didn't hurry on their way, stopping for tea at a wayside cottage before by-passing Colchester and making for Dedham, where Octavia found Le Talbooth to be everything Lucas had promised. They had their drinks by the quiet river running beside the restaurant and then dined leisurely before starting on the last leg of their journey. It was dark by now and there was plenty to interest Octavia as they waited to go aboard, and once in her cabin, she discovered that she was so tired from her long day's travel that a couple of turns on deck was all she needed before saying goodnight to Lucas and going below again. At her cabin door he said: 'I'm next door. If you want anything, don't hesitate to knock me up, and that goes for not being able to sleep, too.'

She looked up into his quiet face. 'You're very good to me, Lucas. I shall do my best to be a splendid wife. Once I'm…in a week or two when I'm more settled, I'll be a better companion. I'm not much good at the moment.'

'You're doing very nicely.' He bent and kissed her cheek lightly and held the door for her. 'I've asked the steward to call you with tea and toast, we can breakfast at home.' His eyes held hers. 'You'll sleep.' It was a statement and she nodded obediently.

'Yes, I'm quite tired.'

The cabin was well appointed. Octavia had a shower and got into her narrow bed and fell asleep within minutes, while she was still wondering how much such extreme comfort cost and did Lucas always travel regardless of expense or was it just because it was their first trip together?

But she forgot that in the excitement of landing the next morning—not that Holland looked so very different to England. Customs sheds were alike the world over, she imagined, but the predominant language now was Dutch and she listened fascinated, wondering if she would ever be able to speak it herself. The police looked different too, and driving away on the wrong side of the road was something else she would have to get used to. Lucas assured her that she would, and quickly, and went on to tell her a little of the countryside they were passing through. They were almost in the outskirts of den Haag when she asked: 'Aren't you excited at the idea of seeing Berendina again?' And before he could reply: 'Does she stay at home while you're away, or have you sisters or brothers?'

'Both, but she stays at home. My housekeeper is devoted to her, and yes, I shall be very happy to see her again. We're great friends—just as you will be with her, Octavia.'

Lucas had swept the car through the heart of the city by now and Octavia had a glimpse of a bustling shopping centre before he turned into Noordeinde and Zeestraat, going towards Scheveningen, but he turned off again before very long and still on the fringe of the city's centre, drove through several narrow streets to reach a quiet square, bisected by a canal and lined with tall narrow houses. Not one of their picturesque gabled roofs resembled its neighbour, but nonetheless they made a harmonious whole and a charming picture. Lucas stopped at a house on one of its corners, a high wall and a narrow passage dividing it from the side of the square adjoining it, and got out to open Octavia's door.

'Oh, is this it?' She gazed around her with interest. 'A flat?' She stared at the magnificent old house. 'It's very large…'

'Not a flat,' he sounded almost apologetic. 'We're lucky, too, because it's on a corner and we have a sizeable garden. The garages are at the back.'

He had helped her out as he spoke and now, with her beside him, trod up the double steps to the elaborately carved door. He just had time to say: 'There may be one or two people to welcome you,' before the door was opened with something of a flourish and a tall, very thin old man greeted them.

'This is Daan,' explained the doctor. 'He was with my father and mother and is an old and trusted friend of the family. He speaks a little English.'

Octavia shook hands and said How do you do with a smile which lighted up the whole of her lovely face, and then the smile changed to a look of utter amazement; standing behind Daan in the roomy vestibule was a small, rotund woman with pepper and salt hair and bright blue eyes. She was flanked on one side by two young women and a youth with a shock of lint white hair, and on her other side stood Charlie and Mrs Stubbs.

'Charlie—Mrs Stubbs?' exclaimed Octavia disbelievingly, and looked at Lucas. His 'Yes, my dear,' was positively soothing as he introduced Juffrouw Hinksma, who made a speech of welcome in her own language, beaming and twinkling as she did so, then Sasje and Ranskje and then, finally, Charlie and Mrs Stubbs.

'I don't understand,' said Octavia in a bewildered voice. 'How did you both get here—in this house…'

'Doctor van der Weijnen, 'e did it—'e needed us, 'e said,' explained Charlie. 'I does the odd jobs around the place and Mrs Stubbs 'ere, she 'elps Juffrouw Hinksma an' does the sewing.' He sighed blissfully. "'Appy, we are, Sister—got a 'ome an' a job.'

'And you and Doctor dear 'as married,' declared Mrs Stubbs with deep satisfaction, 'and a nice pair you'll make. Me and Charlie are ever so 'appy about that—you being married.' Mrs Stubbs beamed at Octavia. 'We 'opes you lives long and happy tergether, the pair of yer, and that nice little daughter of yours, Doctor dear—and 'er brothers and sisters, I've no doubt, given time.'

'Thank you for your good wishes, Mrs Stubbs,' said the doctor gravely, and shook them both by the hand. 'I'm sure that Mevrouw van der Weijnen will very much like having you here. You're both settled in?'

They chorused a delighted agreement as he took Octavia's arm and led her through the big double doors Daan was holding open.

The hall was a splendid apartment; not large but panelled in white-painted wood and with a carved stair-case in one corner. There was an archway beyond leading, Octavia guessed, to the kitchen, and a number of doors on either side. Each door was elaborately carved and surmounted by swags of fruit and flowers in a variety of woods, gilded and coloured, and the ceiling, equally elaborately plastered, had gilded cornices. Octavia could hardly wait to see the rest of the house and when Daan opened one of the doors and Lucas stood aside to let her go in, she wasn't disappointed. The room was panelled too, a dark wood this time with a deep cream silk hanging above it. There was a thick mulberry carpet on the floor and mulberry curtains at the high wide windows. A sitting room, she presumed, looking around her at the comfortable chairs and lamp tables and the two deep, well cushioned sofas each side of the wide stone hearth.

'It's beautiful,' she said softly. 'I had no idea…'

'I'm glad you like it. We'll have a cup of coffee and then Juffrouw Hinksma will take you to your room—we'll have breakfast in half an hour if that suits you?' Lucas glanced at his watch. 'It's not yet nine o'clock. Berendina gets back from school just after midday. I'll stay for lunch with you both, but I have several appointments this afternoon, I'm afraid.'

Octavia found her tongue at last. 'It's not a bit what I expected,' she began. 'I—I thought—well, that you were just a GP with a few beds at the local hospital, but you're not, are you?'

He crossed his long legs and gave her a steady stare. 'No, I'm not, but I can't see that it makes any difference. I'm still a doctor, you know, and just as busy as any GP.'

'Yes, oh, yes—but this house…'

'My home,' he informed her gently, 'handed on from one generation to the next, a responsibility and one which I enjoy.'

Coffee came on a massive silver tray and Octavia poured it carefully from the George the Second coffee pot into delicate china cups, feeling shy and awkward. The fact that she was married to the quiet man sitting opposite her, who seemed to take all this splendour for granted, was borne home to her with a sudden force which left her doubtful as to whether she had been quite right in the head to have even considered marrying him in the first place. Her gloomy thoughts were reflected in her face, although she wasn't aware of this, so that she was considerably taken aback when Lucas observed matter-of-factly: 'Don't worry, Octavia, it's only a perfectly natural reaction—everything will seem quite normal and ordinary again.'

He got up and tugged the embroidered bell pull by the fireplace. 'Juffrouw Hinksma shall take you upstairs and we'll meet for breakfast.' He came over to where she was sitting and pulled her gently to her feet. 'And don't look like that, my dear; I promise it will be all right.'

She managed a smile then and went obediently with the housekeeper, up the staircase to a wide landing above where there were several doors and a number of corridors leading from it. Juffrouw Hinksma opened one of the doors and smilingly ushered her inside, and Octavia went past her into one of the loveliest rooms she had ever been in.

Its furniture was satinwood, inlaid with a design of fruit and flowers in a superb marquetry, offset by the cream and honey-coloured brocade curtains at its two wide windows. The same stiff silk hung at the four-poster bed and had been used as a bedspread, in nice contrast to the pale blue covers on the chairs and the silk hangings above the waist-high panelled walls. Octavia, left alone by the smiling housekeeper, crossed the thick cream carpet to examine the dressing table—Queen Anne, she suspected, with its delicate cabriole legs. It supported a charming mirror with small drawers beneath and she touched it with delicate fingers. 'William and Mary,' she told herself, and went to look behind the three doors in the room. The first was a clothes cupboard, fitted with every conceivable drawer and shelf. It surprised her to see that her things had already been unpacked and put away in it.

The second door led to a bathroom, pale blue tiled and carpeted in cream and furnished with every comfort she could have dreamed up. The third door opened on to a dressing room and from there there was another door in the further wall which, when she poked her inquisitive head through it, took her back into the corridor again. Aware that she had wasted enough time as it was, she had a shower and presently, fresh and exquisitely neat once more, she went downstairs.

Lucas was in the hall, leaning against a wall, reading a newspaper but he came to meet her as she went down the staircase with a cheerful: 'I'm famished, aren't you?' and walked her to a door at the back of the hall and opened it.

The room they entered was small and furnished solidly with Biedermeier chairs arranged at a round table, decked now with a crisp linen cloth, blue and white china and plain, beautifully polished silver. Moreover, there was a small bright fire in the steel grate and as they sat themselves down Charlie sidled in behind them. 'Tea or coffee, guv'nor?' he wanted to know, and then corrected himself with: 'And you, ma'am, of course.' He added in a friendly voice: 'The coffee's a bit of all right 'ere.'

They settled for coffee and when he had gone Octavia said anxiously: 'Oh, dear, do you mind being called "Guv'nor"? Perhaps he's not quite—what I mean is, what about Daan and Juffrouw Hinksma and the others? Do they get on well?'

'Excellently. Besides, he's quick to learn despite his age.' He smiled at her. 'Have some toast?'

She took a piece and buttered it. 'It was kind of you to give Charlie a chance, and Mrs Stubbs, too.'

He was sugaring his coffee. 'Juffrouw Hinksma needed a little more help and Daan is delighted to have someone to boss around.'

Octavia bit into her toast and discovered that she was hungry. 'I have a most beautiful room—I didn't know that you had such a lovely house.'

'I'm glad you like it—we'll go over it when I have the time, or better still, Berendina shall act as your guide. You like old houses?' He began to talk about its building and history, putting her at ease, making her feel that she belonged there and that it wasn't just a dream. But he couldn't stay long; presently he got to his feet, saying that he had patients to see and how would she like to spend an hour in the sitting room where she would find the English newspapers. So she bade him a rather more cheerful goodbye than she felt and went with him across the hall once more into yet another room, a good deal larger than the breakfast room had been but just as comfortable, secretly dismayed that she would have to meet Berendina without him. But in this she was mistaken, for at the door he turned to tell her: 'I'll contrive to leave the hospital in time to fetch Berendina and bring her back with me.'

'Oh—thank you. Does she know about me—us?'

'Yes, I telephoned her from Alresford.'

When he had gone Octavia got up and wandered round the room, looking at pictures and picking up the charming silver and porcelain ornaments on its tables and shelves, but there weren't any photos. She had expected to see at least one or two of the little girl, and possibly one of Lucas's dead wife, although perhaps he had arranged for those to be laid aside in case she was upset at seeing them. She had no reason to be upset, she told herself; it wasn't as if she were in love with Lucas. He had been a tower of strength and he had been very kind on the cruise, he had also been ill-tempered and a little arrogant—very much accustomed to having his own way; she would have to remember that. His house was obviously well run and by the look of things he was liked by his staff, and it had been generous of him to employ Mrs Stubbs and Charlie. Her thoughts were interrupted by him now, wanting to know if she wanted anything and to tell her that Daan would be bringing her coffee in half an hour if that suited her.

So the morning passed and didn't drag at all because first one and then the other came in on some excuse or other; Mrs Stubbs to ask after the patients she had left at Maud's, Daan to discover, in his sparse English, if there was anything at all Octavia required and then Charlie with Juffrouw Hinksma, of whom he obviously stood in considerable awe and for whom he meekly translated while she enjoyed a little chat with her new mistress. It seemed as though they had conspired together to keep her occupied until lunchtime, and indeed she had been alone barely ten minutes when she heard the great front door open and Lucas's voice answering a shrill excited voice. She got up from her chair and stood nervously, watching the door, her good looks all but blotted out by sheer fright.

The door opened and Lucas stood there, one arm round the small shoulders of his daughter, a flaxen-haired child with his eyes and nose, his good looks, softened to prettiness in her little face. 'Hullo,' he said, and smiled across the room at Octavia, seeing her white face and tense look. 'Isn't it nice to have someone to come home to, Berendina? This is Octavia exactly as you wished—pretty and young and not in the least severe.'

The child left him and ran across the room to Octavia and held out a hand. 'I am glad,' she said in halting English, 'you are as Papa tells me,' she put her head on one side, studying Octavia, 'but you are perhaps more pretty, but I like your face. You will be kind to me?'

Octavia had forgotten that Lucas was there. She bent down and kissed the child's cheek and squeezed the little hand in hers. 'We are going to be very happy together, Berendina, and I'll promise always to be kind to you…'

'And to Papa?'

Octavia shot a glance at him, still standing by the door. 'Yes,' she said steadily, 'and to Papa.'

Lucas had left the door as she spoke and was strolling towards them. 'Such an important occasion calls for a celebration. I have no patients until this evening, so shall we go out after lunch? How about taking you both to Scheveningen for tea? Berendina, shall we not show Octavia our Kurhaus and perhaps a walk along the boulevard to get an appetite first?'

They discussed the afternoon's outing over a gay lunch, and Octavia, watching Berendina giggling and chattering away to her father and then meeting the child's friendly eyes, realised that even though she had lost her father, she had gained a family to fill his place in her life. For the first time since his death she felt a surge of interest in what was going on around her; life no longer seemed aimless; she joined in the lighthearted conversation with unforced pleasure.

Hours later, lying in her enormous luxurious bed, Octavia remembered the afternoon and the evening which had followed it. It had been fun driving to Scheveningen, walking by the sea with Berendina between them holding their hands and talking non-stop and then, later, the tea, with everything a small girl could wish for in the Kurhaus. Lucas had been a delightful companion to them both and although it was early days yet, Octavia sensed that the child liked her, just as she had felt an instant liking for Berendina. And in the evening while Lucas was with his patients she had accompanied the child upstairs to her bedroom to admire her dolls and toys in the vast cupboard against one of its walls. She was taken to see the nursery too, a roomy, comfortably shabby apartment, peaceful and secure. Octavia, obligingly rocking the rocking horse for Berendina, thought it would be a lovely place for a baby, with its great brass fireguard in front of the old-fashioned grate, its comfortable easy chairs and sturdy table.

'I'm too big to sleep in the night nursery now,' declared her companion, 'but of course I play here. Papa played here too and my *tantes* and *Oom Kees*, and they slept in the night nurseries too, with a nanny. I haven't a nanny, but I had a Miss. She was *erg gemeene…*' She paused to see if Octavia had understood and translated patiently: 'Very mean.' She grinned engagingly. 'I hate her and she goes.'

'Well, don't hate me,' begged Octavia, 'because I don't want to go.'

Berendina flung an arm round her neck. 'But of course you will not go—Papa would not allow it. Besides, you are my mama now, and mamas don't leave their children.' She added with fervour: 'I wish that you will have babies.'

The thought struck Octavia that she rather agreed with the wish. The house was enormous, it could absorb a dozen children easily. Rather too many, of course, but four perhaps? She shook her head to shake away the daydream; Lucas had made it clear enough that he cherished no ideas about a family—or a wife, for that matter. She was to run his house, entertain his guests, be his companion when he wanted her company and be a mother to Berendina.

They had gone back to the child's bedroom presently and when she was tucked up in bed and kissed goodnight, Octavia had gone to her own room to tidy herself and change her suit for a plain wool dress, keeping her mind strictly on the day's events. It would do her no good to harp back to her former life in England. She had burned her boats and now she came to think about it, they hadn't been such safe ones either.

And later she and Lucas dined, this time in a magnificent room panelled in dark oak with a table which could seat a dozen or more with comfort. The place mats were lace and the glass and silver shone and sparkled with age and meticulous care, although Octavia couldn't remember what they had eaten. Lucas had talked in a casual friendly manner about his work and afterwards they had spent a pleasant hour in the drawing room, talking in a comfortable placid way, a conversation she would have liked to have prolonged, but when he mentioned the work waiting for him in his study she had pleaded tiredness and gone at once to her room. She would have to remember not to intrude into his life. She wondered sleepily about his friends; he must have quite a few, judging by the pile of letters waiting for him when they had arrived that morning, and the telephone had been ringing on and off all day. There was a great deal to find out about him; he had told her almost nothing. She would have to find out for herself. She slept on the resolve.

Two days passed during which she saw very little of Lucas. He had already left on the first morning when she got down to breakfast with Berendina and although he was home in the evening, he had to go out again directly after dinner. And on the second morning she had gone down to breakfast early, only to find the door closing on his broad back as she started down the staircase. She might have felt like a guest and nothing more if it hadn't been for Berendina, but luckily that child had strong ideas about mothers. Octavia took her to school and fetched her and was conscious that it was a matter of pride to her small stepdaughter that she should do so. She was introduced to several small boys and girls and felt secretly that she was being shown off. That Berendina had been lonely was very evident and Octavia's heart warmed to the child's efforts to integrate her into the household. She was advised what to do at every turn and ruthlessly questioned, sometimes embarrassingly so. 'My friend Klara,' pronounced Berendina thoughtfully, 'her mama and papa only have one bedroom between them, but you and papa have one each. Why?'

Octavia bent her head to remove an invisible thread

from her skirt, thanking heaven that she had some sort of an answer, although it was painful for her to utter it. 'My father died just a very little while ago, darling, and so I feel—not ill, exactly—' She didn't have to go on, for Berendina chimed in!

'Poor Mama!' She flung her arms round Octavia's shoulders. 'He would have been my *opa*.'

Octavia tried not to feel sad. 'Yes, darling—he would have liked that very much.'

'You have a photo of him? I may have one to put on table in my room? He is my grandfather still, *nietwaar?*'

And that afternoon, when Lucas came in for tea, Berendina, just back from school with Octavia, went to perch beside him with the urgent request that Mama should be taken out and bought new clothes. 'They are nice, what she wears, but she must have many more—like Klara's mama.'

Lucas looked surprised and then laughed. 'What a shocking husband I am! Octavia always seems nicely dressed to me, but I'm sure you are right, *liefje*, she shall have all the new clothes she wants.' He looked across at Octavia, sitting opposite and rather pink in the face. 'I'll open accounts for you at several shops—my God, you haven't any money either, have you? I'll get things settled tomorrow morning and you can go shopping whenever you wish.'

Octavia, his sharp eyes on her, suddenly felt very conscious of last year's skirts. 'Thank you, but I have quite a lot of clothes…'

'Not enough for our daughter it seems. I'll open an account for you at my bank.' He mentioned the sum and she gaped at him.

'But I couldn't possibly take all that—it's a fortune.'

He said blandly: 'No, it's not, and shortly you will need

plenty of clothes—there will be entertaining and visits. Besides, the winter will be cold—you will need thick things!' He turned to Berendina. 'Isn't that so, poppet? And you must have new clothes, too. I expect to see you both very smart.'

It was as they sat over their after-dinner coffee on the second day that Lucas remarked casually: 'I think it is a good idea if we all go up to Friesland to my father. I'm free this weekend—we'll go after breakfast on Saturday; you'll like him.' He passed his cup for more coffee. 'You are settling down, Octavia? There is no need to ask if you and Berendina get on, because that is obvious, but you are happy?'

She handed him his cup. 'Yes, Lucas, thank you. Everyone is so kind and Charlie and Mrs Stubbs are so helpful. I've been round the house with Juffrouw Hinksma and Daan has shown me the silver and explained the routine.'

She was careful to keep reproach out of her voice; she had wanted to see the house in his company and Lucas had forgotten or had no time, perhaps. She had had to keep her delight to herself, merely uttering formal phrases to the housekeeper, while she longed to exclaim over the beautiful rooms and their contents, and especially did she want to know about the numerous paintings and portraits in every room; Lucas's ancestors, but they could just as well have been strangers, just as he was a stranger.

'Your father—whereabouts in Friesland does he live?'

'To the east of Leeuwarden—we have a house there and now that he has retired he prefers the peace and quiet.'

'He was a doctor here?'

'Yes.' It seemed that he wasn't going to tell her any more; possibly he found her questions tedious. 'I shall enjoy it,' she told him quietly, and because he had picked up a sheaf of papers, went early to bed.

She consulted Berendina the next morning over their breakfast. 'What shall I wear?' she wanted to know, because Berendina took a great interest in her wardrobe, such as it was.

'Something new,' cried the little girl. 'You will go this morning and choose—this afternoon too, I am to eat my midday meal with Klara, had you forgotten, because it is her birthday, so you can also spend all day until school ends.'

'Well, all right, darling, but I'll come and fetch you at half past three as usual. Your papa has a lecture to give, so he won't be home either.'

Octavia had a list of the shops where she had an account as well as a roll of notes in her purse. The day was fine with a keen wind bringing the first breath of winter, even though it was only October. Octavia hurried along, primed by an obliging Charlie as to which way to go; he, it seemed, had lost no time in making himself at home in the city. She was making for Metz, a department store which Mrs Stubbs assured her was classy, and when she had looked around her there and got a little used to the prices, she could always go farther afield to the boutiques and dress shops on the Plaats.

It was all much easier than she had anticipated, too. Everyone spoke English for a start, and there was a wonderful selection of clothes. She found a corduroy suit at Metz in a rich russet, found too a silk shirt blouse in a rich cream to go with it and then, quite carried away, a cashmere sweater, fine and soft and wickedly expensive. She had coffee then and wandered off to the Plaats where she discovered a scarf which exactly suited the outfit, and then a handbag and gloves. Delighted with her purchases, she wandered into the Bistroqued, quite lost but not minding in the least, and ate her lunch.

It seemed sensible to take a taxi back, as she had no idea where to go and a great many parcels to carry, and still elated with her shopping, she rang the bell for Daan, who tutted at the sight of her so overburdened and took everything from her as she went in. 'Mrs Stubbs shall take these to your room, *mevrouw*,' he told her tolerantly. 'I will bring coffee to the small sitting room, you will be in need of refreshment.'

She beamed at him, 'Oh, thank you, Daan. The doctor isn't home, I suppose?'

'No, *mevrouw*—I believe that he is to be late.'

She felt disappointment well up inside her. She wanted to share her pleasure with someone; she wanted to tell him, too, that the sharp edge of her grief had been dulled; she was still sad, but she could bear it now.

She went into the sitting room, drank a cup of the coffee which Daan brought and then went to the great Italian Baroque mirror. It was of limewood, elaborately carved, and she paused to admire it before studying her own reflection. She had cast off her hat and her hair was a little untidy, but her face had colour again. She added a little more lipstick and went back to the cheerful fire. She was warming her hands when she heard the door behind her open. Lucas—home early; there was an hour before she needed to fetch Berendina, so perhaps they could talk. She began eagerly: 'I didn't expect you so soon. I've been shopping. I'm afraid everything cost an awful lot of money—I got carried away…'

But the voice which answered hers wasn't Lucas's. Its gay 'And why not—that's what money's for,' sent her whizzing round to face a young man standing in the doorway. A member of the van der Weijnen family without a doubt; there was the nose, the blue eyes, only the mouth wasn't firm as Lucas's was, and he was a head shorter.

'Who are you?' she demanded.

He came across the room and stopped in front of her. 'Marcus—cousin to your esteemed husband. I heard here and there that he had brought a bride back with him and I wanted to see you for myself. So secret of him, but only to be expected, all things considered.' He grinned engagingly and held out a hand. 'Am I forgiven for taking you by surprise?'

She took his hand and said with gentle dignity: 'If you are Lucas's cousin then I am glad to meet you.'

He really had a most engaging smile. 'What—no cousinly kiss?'

She had to smile back at him even while she shook her head; she was saved from replying by the opening door, and this time it was Lucas.

CHAPTER SEVEN

OCTAVIA had the instant impression that Lucas was annoyed, only to banish it immediately at his pleasant: 'Marcus—what brings you here?'

The two men shook hands and Marcus laughed—he laughed a lot, she reflected. 'Rumour, Lucas, rumour. I was at Uncle's home a few days ago and he had your telephone message while I was there. Naturally, I was all agog to see the bride. Why the secrecy, *jongen*?'

'No secrecy,' Lucas's voice was cool and faintly amused. 'You must know by now that I'm not a man to shout his affairs from the housetops.' He walked past his cousin and took Octavia's hand and kissed her deliberately. 'I had the chance to come home early, my dear,' he told her placidly. 'I thought we might go together and fetch Berendina.'

'Oh, nice. She'll love that. We'll walk?'

'Why not? We can take Whiskey with us.' Whiskey was the golden labrador, elderly and much loved, and as though he had heard his name, Daan opened the door and the dog came in to greet his master, wag a tail gently at sight of Octavia and ignore Marcus.

'Good lord, still got that old wreck?' Marcus said it kindly enough, but Octavia answered him quite sharply with:

'He's not a wreck, even if he is old. He's one of the family.'

'Just as you are, Cousin Octavia?' His voice was mocking, but before she could answer Lucas said smoothly:

'Just as Octavia is.' He added on a faintly questioning note: 'Did you want to see me, Marcus? If not, may we beg to be excused? There are certain matters we have to discuss and we don't see so very much of each other.'

Marcus laughed again. 'I can take a hint. Are we going to have a family gathering to meet the bride?'

'Certainly—and of course you will come. We shall be delighted to see you, shall we not, Octavia?'

The blue eyes stared down into hers and she wondered at their intentness. 'Of course; I'm looking forward to meeting your family, Lucas.' She smiled at Marcus. 'It was nice of you to call,' she assured him, and held out her hand.

Marcus accepted his dismissal with good grace, saying cheerfully that he would be sure to visit them very shortly. 'Don't imagine you can keep Octavia hidden away, Lucas,' he declared, half laughing. 'I wish I'd seen her first!'

Which piece of nonsense Octavia ignored; she wanted him to go quickly so that she could tell Lucas about her shopping—and what were the certain matters to discuss? She frowned a little and Lucas asked: 'Did he annoy you? He's one of the more extrovert types in the family.'

'No, not in the least—I thought he was rather nice. He's a lot younger than you, isn't he?' She was plumping up a cushion as she spoke and didn't see her husband's face.

'He's twenty-eight,' Lucas told her. 'And what have you done with your day?'

She turned to him eagerly. 'Oh, I went shopping. I—I needed something to wear when we go to visit your father…'

He had picked up the newspaper lying on the coffee

table. 'Good, I'm sure it will be charming,' he told her idly, and glanced at the clock. 'We don't need to fetch Berendina just yet, do we?'

He sat himself down opposite her and opened his paper, and she was conscious of disappointment. She had wanted him to take some interest in her new outfit, but apparently he couldn't care less. She said hesitantly: 'You said there were things to discuss…'

He glanced up. 'Did I? Just a way of getting rid of Marcus. I've had a busy morning and his youthful exuberance exhausts me.'

'That makes you sound positively middle-aged!' She had meant it as a joke and it was disconcerting when he replied calmly:

'But I am, Octavia.'

She looked at him then, appalled. 'Oh, I didn't mean it—you mustn't say that, even think it…not even as a joke.'

He said quietly: 'You were joking, Octavia.'

'I'm sorry.' She stared down at his face, its blandness like a wall between them, wondering why she should mind so much. 'Lucas,' she tried again, 'I've never thought of your age—never once—you're just you.' She added desperately: 'Do you understand what I mean?'

He smiled at her although his eyes were searching. 'If you make many more pretty speeches like that one, I shall get an inflated ego!'

And somehow, she saw very little of him after that—not alone, at any rate; there was always Berendina there, chattering happily, content with her little life, and when she had gone to bed, Lucas pleaded work to do or a patient to visit. And yet he was kindness itself and a splendid companion when they were together, only he never talked about anything personal. Octavia still had no idea as to his work or when or how his wife had died; she didn't even know her name. It was as though Lucas intended to shut her out of his private life, although on the surface they got on extraordinarily well. And on the Saturday morning when she joined him at breakfast with Berendina clinging to her arm, he admired the new outfit. He did it with such fervour that she looked suspiciously at him and wanted to know why he was being so very complimentary.

'Well, my dear,' he said with mock humility, 'Berendina threatened the direst punishment for me if I didn't.' Which made her laugh, something she hadn't done so wholeheartedly for quite some time.

They were going to a small village, explained Lucas, as with Berendina and Whiskey on the back seat and Octavia beside him, he drove the Rolls north out of den Haag. 'It's close to Oostermeer, that's a large village between two lakes. Fanejwoude is just a handful of houses and a church, but it's only fifteen kilometres or so from Leeuwarden. We'll go through Heemstede and Haarlem and take the coast road from there as far as Alkmaar—we turn off there for the Afsluitdijk and Friesland.'

'And coffee, Papa,' chipped in Berendina, 'don't forget coffee at the Lido. For Octavia that will be a splendid place; everyone will see her new clothes!'

Octavia smoothed her velvet skirt with a nicely gloved hand and Lucas laughed. He sounded happy and young and she was aware of her pleasure that he should be. She laughed a little too and assured them that she could hardly wait.

The Lido at Noordwijk-aan-zee was all that a girl would wish for—luxurious surroundings and, as Berendina had said, plenty of people to see the new outfit, and with the added bonus of a splendid view of the sea, but they didn't stay long. They were due for lunch and even in the Rolls they needed an hour and a half to get there. They had come no distance at all and there were Heemstede and Haarlem to get through and Alkmaar still half an hour's drive away. And a charming drive it was, through woods and dunes, though far too short, for in no time at all they were through Alkmaar and tearing cross-country towards the Afsluitdijk, but even on this road there was a great deal to see and Lucas to point out anything of interest as they went. Octavia enjoyed every minute of it until, through Leeuwarden, Lucas slowed the car through country lanes running between flat meadows full of cattle.

The village, when they reached it, was indeed small; no more than a scattering of cottages and a very large church, and on its outer perimeter his father's house; solid and square and perhaps, thought Octavia, not very beautiful, not on the outside at any rate. But inside was different, with a large, square hall with enormous doors and a polished floor across which they were led by a tall, strongly built woman of uncertain age, introduced by Lucas as Lottie. The room they entered seemed vast, with tremendous windows swathed in velvet drapes, and a carpet which covered almost the whole of its floor. The furniture was massive too, matching the stone hearth in which burned a cheerful fire. The only occupant of the room rose to his feet as they went in, booming a welcome in a strong voice. Lucas's parent, although he was an old man, still retained his son's good looks.

He embraced Berendina, grasped his son's hand and turned to Octavia.

'My daughter-in-law!' he exclaimed in English as excellent as his son's. 'I welcome you into the family with the greatest pleasure. You are just as beautiful as Lucas said you were.' He bent to kiss her cheek and then turned to Berendina. 'It is delightful to have so charming a mama, is it not, *liefje*?'

Berendina broke into a spate of Dutch and then switched back to English. 'I have not the words,' she explained to Octavia, 'but I say only nice things about you to Opa and he likes your new suit.' She turned back to her grandparent. 'I am also to have new clothes; Papa has said so.'

Lucas laughed. 'I'm outnumbered, Vader, they're in league against me, but I must say that I like it.'

His father gave a rumbling laugh and asked: 'You will give a reception, of course? The family and our friends?'

They were all sitting, sipping the drinks Lucas had poured, while Berendina sucked lemonade through straws. 'Yes—I thought next week, some time. You will come, naturally, and spend the night. I must telephone the others, too. Saturday might suit everyone and give us time to get things arranged. There will be about eighty of us, I should suppose.'

Octavia tried not to look startled; she had expected to meet Lucas's family sooner or later, but all his friends at once? Her feelings had shown on her face, for Lucas said placidly: 'You'll enjoy it, Octavia. Besides, what a splendid excuse for you and Berendina to go shopping.'

'Of course no one has met Octavia yet?'

'Marcus called, Vader, and introduced himself to Octavia...'

The older man grunted. 'With Marcus, that is to be expected.' He was going to say more, but was interrupted by Lottie, who opened the door to usher in a tall young woman and say with the familiarity of an old servant: '*Hier is uwe dochter, mijnheer.*'

Both men got up to greet her and Berendina rushed to cross the room and fling herself at her aunt, while Octavia took stock of her sister-in-law—very pretty, tall and slim and fair-haired, with sparkling blue eyes. She got up as Lucas went over to her with his sister and smiled back at her. 'Octavia, this is Lucilla, my eldest sister. She is married to a surgeon who has a practice in Groningen—he can't get here for lunch, but you will meet him next week.'

They had barely had time to exchange a handful of words before the door was opened again and Lottie appeared once more, this time ushering in two girls. '*Nog twee*,' she announced as they joined the others gathered round the fire.

There were more introductions: Ganna, the older of the two, was much the same age as Octavia and very like her elder sister, but the younger was darker and smaller in build with bright blue eyes which twinkled engagingly. She was several years younger than her sisters and, Octavia suspected, the pet of the family. She threw her arms round Lucas's neck and kissed him soundly, kissed Berendina too and then put out both hands to Octavia. 'I know all about you,' she declared gaily, 'and you're even prettier than Lucas said. It's lovely to have you in the family. My name's Jellina.' She kissed Octavia on the cheek. 'What good fortune that Lucas has found you, you're just right.' She nodded in a satisfied way, for all the world as though she had arranged the match herself, and then turned her head to ask Lucas: 'Where is Eilof?'

He gave her a lazy smile and offered her sherry. 'Coming. It was Vader's idea that Octavia should meet us here, before any of the rest of the family.'

He had come to stand by Octavia's chair. Now he sat down on its arm and threw an arm round her shoulders, and she quelled an absurd desire to put up her hand and slip it into his. Instead she gave him a quick, shy glance, to find him staring down at her with curious intentness. 'A little overpowering, aren't we?' he asked easily. 'But I promise you that Eilof will be the last of us—today, at any rate. Here he is now.'

Eilof was young, still in his early twenties and bearing his brother's good looks. He kissed her heartily, exchanged brotherly greetings with his sisters, tossed Berendina in the air and then went to speak to his father. He was nice, thought Octavia, and so were all three sisters. She went in to lunch presently nicely warmed by their open friendliness.

The afternoon went swiftly. Octavia was borne on an inspection of the house after lunch with Berendina clinging to her hand and all three sisters accompanying them. By the time they had looked over the old house they were firm friends and tea was a noisy, cheerful meal. Not at all what she had expected, she had to admit to herself; she had thought that Lucas was a man who preferred to live quietly, but among his own family he was evidently regarded with great affection, although it was just as obvious that he was the eldest and as such was consulted and deferred to. Not that he took advantage of this, indeed it pleased her to see that he in his turn showed a proper respect for his father, who despite his age, was still very much the head of the family. They all parted on the best of terms and went their various ways, promising to meet again on the following Saturday. Lucas was the last to leave and as they bade the old man goodbye Octavia was touched to hear him say: 'I was sorry to hear about your father, Octavia. I should have liked to have known him. You must allow me to do my poor best to replace him.'

She had been unable to answer him, although she had leaned up and kissed him.

Lucas was home on Sunday, and although it was a chilly, grey day with a faint drizzle, they all went to Scheveningen, to walk for miles along the shore, with Berendina tearing ahead of them and Whiskey taking his time behind. Octavia loved every minute of it even though the wind tore through her raincoat as though it had been made of paper so that she shivered a little, but when Lucas asked her if she were cold she declared that no, she wasn't, not in the least, for fear he should bring their walk to an end.

The next day he came home unexpectedly to lunch, giving it his intention to drive Berendina back to school afterwards and fetch her that afternoon. 'I have no patients until this evening,' he observed. 'Octavia, you'll come too, of course?'

She agreed readily; school was a bare ten minutes' walk away, in the car it would be a matter of a couple of minutes and hardly seemed worth the ride. She added tentatively: 'Walking is healthy…'

'Oh, very.' His glance mocked her gently. 'But we have some shopping to do.'

A remark which set Berendina off asking questions in her own language, all of which must have received satisfactory answers, because she went to kiss her father, whooping with delight about something. Octavia, watching, wondered if it were the little girl's birthday and they were to buy her present. It seemed likely, especially as Lucas caught her eye over his daughter's head and remarked easily: 'I'll tell you later.'

They had dropped Berendina at the school gates and he was actually parking the car in a narrow side street close to Noordeinde when he told her.

'Shopping, Octavia; you must have a warm raincoat, something lined with a hood. I thought we might go into the Bonneterie and see if there's anything you like.'

The prices appalled her. To pay so much for a mere raincoat…but when she whispered this to Lucas, sitting at his ease while she was shown a variety of garments, he only smiled and told her not to look at the price tags. So she didn't, finally choosing a warmly lined rainproof coat with a hood which could be fastened tight under her pretty chin, and when she had finally completed the business and would have left the luxurious shop he turned her the other way with a casual: 'While we're here, you might as well look at some dresses—Saturday, you know. And by the way, I have promised Berendina that we would bring her here after school. She will stay up for dinner and wishes to dazzle all eyes. You don't mind?'

'Me, mind?' asked Octavia, much astonished. 'You're her father, Lucas.'

He turned to look at her. 'And you are her mother, my dear.'

She found herself smiling at him. 'Oh, yes, and I am enjoying it—you have no idea…she's a darling, just like…' She stopped just in time and went red at his amused:

'All right, I won't ask. Here's the gown department. Get anything which takes your fancy, but personally I like you in pink.'

She found exactly what she wanted, but then who wouldn't when they had no need to ask the price? Soft pink organza over silk with a scooped-out neckline and ballooning sleeves ending just above the elbows and tied with darker pink velvet. The skirt was full, with a pleated ruffle round its hem, and it fitted perfectly. Octavia went to show it to Lucas, a little diffident but his approval was so sincere that she blossomed under it and when he suggested new slippers to go with the gown, she made no demur.

They walked back to the car then and Lucas suggested tea before they went to fetch Berendina: 'For you'll need it,' he pointed out, half-laughing. 'Our daughter is all female when it comes to choosing a party dress.'

Her heart lifted at the 'our'—it was nice to belong, even

though it seemed that she was to belong more to Berendina than to him. She agreed happily as they walked through to Noordeinde and the Maison Krul, where over tea and the richest éclairs she had ever seen they discussed the forthcoming reception. Not that there was much to discuss, as it was plain to her that Lucas knew exactly what needed to be done and ordered and was only deferring to her as the housewife whose business it really was. It crossed her mind suddenly that he had been—was still being—thoughtful and kind, cushioning her against her new life until she was used to it, keeping her occupied too so that she had little time to grieve. She spoke her thoughts aloud.

'I'll never be able to thank you, Lucas. I've only just realised how good you are to me—I feel as though I've got a protective wall around me…' Her beautiful eyes searched his across the elegant little table.

He didn't smile, only looked at her thoughtfully. 'You're worth protecting,' he told her quietly, and then: 'Shall we go? Or Berendina will be beside herself with impatience.'

They spent another half an hour in the Bonneterie later while the little girl tried on party frocks. She knew what she wanted, but she was very willing for Octavia to give advice, eager, pathetically so—to show the salesgirl that she had a mama to help her decide. Between them they finally picked on a rich brown velvet with a lace collar and cuffs to the short sleeves, explaining to Lucas that dark colours were all the fashion for little girls and then joining forces to wheedle a pair of bronze slippers out of him. A highly enjoyable afternoon, considered Octavia as she tucked up her small stepdaughter for the night, marred now by the fact that Lucas had just been called to the hospital to anaesthetise a tricky case. She waited up for him after dinner, but he didn't come home.

The week went quickly by and although she knew very

little about the running of the big house, Octavia found that she was consulted about this that and the other thing at every turn. Should they have water ices as well as the superb trifle Juffrouw Hinksma was planning? Should Charlie take the gentlemen's coats at the door or would he be more useful behind the scenes, and which bedroom should be allocated for the ladies? And when that was decided would it be a good idea if Mrs Stubbs stationed herself there ready to give any help needed, thus leaving Juffrouw Hinksma free to rule over her kitchen? Octavia, kept busy, hardly noticed the lack of time Lucas spent in his house; she supposed he was extra busy at the hospital or that he had more patients than usual to see. She would have liked to have asked, but he had never volunteered information about his work and somehow she didn't like to enquire. She tried, like a good wife, to keep the petty worries of the household from him, see that he ate the food he liked and that there was always a meal ready for him when he did get home.

But he was free for the weekend; they all had breakfast together, Berendina chattering away in Dutch and English about the evening ahead. It was Lucas who suggested that he might take her out for an hour or two that morning and leave the way clear for Octavia to put the finishing touches to her preparations. That there was practically nothing to do was something she didn't tell him, because then he might have felt that he must ask her to go with them and it seemed likely that he would like to have his small daughter to himself for a little while. So she agreed at once, and when they had gone, repaired to the small sitting room, out of the way of the servants, for as Charlie had said when he met her in the hall, looking for something to do: 'We're all managing very nicely, ma'am—just enough of us, there is, an' we all knows wot we 'as ter do.' And if that wasn't a broad hint, Octavia would have liked to know what was.

She had been there for half an hour, aimlessly looking through the newspaper, when Daan opened the door. 'Here is Mijnheer Marcus van der Weijnen.' His voice was faintly disapproving. 'Shall I ask him to come in, *mevrouw*?'

Her eager: 'Oh, yes, please, Daan,' as she jumped up must have pleased Marcus, hard on the old man's heels, although all he said was:

'I happened to be close by and thought perhaps Lucas was home. May I beg a cup of coffee from you…'

'Well, of course you can. Daan, please would you let us have coffee here?' She turned to her visitor. 'Do sit down, Marcus. Lucas has taken Berendina out for a while and there's just nothing for me to do—everything has been done and Juffrouw Hinksma is such a splendid housekeeper.'

'Ah, yes—the preparations for this evening. Are you scared?' He laughed across at her and she wished, fleetingly, that Lucas would sometimes laugh like that. He had done so with his family, but somehow never with her.

'A little,' she admitted, 'but I met Lucas's father and brother and sisters at the weekend, so not everyone will be a stranger.'

'I'm not a stranger, I hope, Octavia.' He sounded friendly and a little concerned. 'I expect you find us a bit overwhelming. You married so quickly—I mean, before you had had the time to meet any of the family.'

She bent to pour the coffee Daan had brought in. 'Well, I expect you know—my father died rather suddenly and—and there wasn't much point in waiting.' She paused. 'Lucas saw to everything—he was wonderful; kind and sympathetic. He understood—he lost his mother…'

Marcus nodded. 'And he adored her.'

'And his wife.' She hadn't meant to say that.

'Margriet? I should hardly say that he adored her—affection, perhaps.' He shrugged. 'She was a pretty creature with nothing behind her lovely face. I imagine that her preoccupation with trivialities drove Lucas mad, and of course having Berendina was the last straw for her—she hated having her. She must have given Lucas a pretty bad time of it, but he never said a word—not to a soul.'

Octavia put down her coffee cup, very pink in the face. 'Of course he wouldn't—he's a good man, and I think he would be angry if he knew that you had spoken of his first wife like that. I don't want to hear any more!'

'About what, my dear?' asked Lucas from the door. 'You look magnificently angry about something.' He didn't wait for her to answer him but turned to Marcus. 'Did you come to see me? You could have said so when we met outside when I left the house.' His voice was very placid. 'And what scandal have you been shocking Octavia with?'

Octavia had got to her feet. 'Oh, he wasn't shocking me, not really—it was just some nonsense.' She smiled at them both, although her eyes still sparkled with anger. 'I'll get Daan to bring some fresh coffee and go and see what Berendina is doing.' She whisked herself out of the room and presently, when she got back with the little girl, it was to find that Marcus had gone and Lucas was sitting, in his great chair, his long legs stretched out before him, apparently asleep.

But he wasn't. Without opening them he said: 'Berendina, will you go down to Juffrouw Hinksma and ask if the cake has come and then find Mrs Stubbs and make quite sure that she knows what to do this evening—oh, and tell Daan that I'll be along presently to see about the drinks.' He repeated it all in Dutch, then opened his eyes and got to his feet. 'Sit here, my dear,' he begged Octavia, and drew forward a small crinoline chair to face his, and then: 'And now tell me what Marcus said to upset you.'

She met his enquiring gaze very directly. 'I wanted to tell you—we were talking about—about Margriet. At least, Marcus was telling me about her, but you mustn't be angry with him. I—I wanted to know…'

He said very quietly: 'But you didn't like what you heard?'

She shook her head. 'It seemed unfair, but you see, I… it was my fault for asking in the first place.'

'You could have asked me, Octavia.'

'I did want to, but I thought you didn't want me to.'

'You didn't mind asking Marcus, though.'

'Well, no—he was friendly and one of those people it's easy to ask questions of, if you see what I mean—and he's family.'

'And young.' Lucas's voice was very even. 'About your age, Octavia.'

She stared back at him, not knowing quite what to say. She could sense his anger, but there was something else too. 'I'm very sorry, Lucas—I shouldn't have pried; you've been so good to me and I had no right. I hope…'

She was interrupted by Berendina, returning from her errands and full of excited chatter. She and Lucas would have to finish their talk later, although she wondered uneasily if he would want that. Somehow she felt that he was going to leave it at that—and most unsatisfactory, too, she thought crossly.

They weren't alone together for the rest of the day, not until the evening, when, with Berendina dressed and gone down to the kitchen to show off her finery, Octavia went down herself to have another quick look at the dining table. She and Juffrouw Hinksma and Mrs Stubbs had spent a good part of the afternoon over it, but there might be something they had overlooked. But there wasn't. She sighed with pleasure at the sight of it, snowy damask, shining silver and glass and a charming centrepiece of pink roses. She hurried across the hall and peeped in at the drawing room too. Its double doors thrown open to the library beyond so that there would be plenty of room for their guests. She didn't hear Lucas; she didn't know he was there until his hand closed over hers on the door handle and his voice said in her ear: 'Quite perfect, my dear.'

She supposed it was relief that he wasn't angry any more that gave her such a thrill of pleasure. She looked up at him over her shoulder, smiling. 'It does look gorgeous. I'm glad you're pleased, Lucas.'

'You look gorgeous too.' He turned her round to get a better look at her. 'That dress suits you very well. It seems the right moment to give you these.' He left her for a moment and picked up a velvet case from one of the wall tables in the hall. 'The family diamonds. I had the ring altered to fit and you must decide which of the other pieces you wish to wear.'

He had opened the case and her delighted eyes sparkled at the contents. A ring, a magnificent stone set in a circle of smaller diamonds; pearl drop earrings set in a diamond cluster; a necklace of diamond clusters which she took to be Georgian in design and a matching bracelet.

She said on an excited breath: 'May I wear the ring? So that we're engaged, you see.'

He slipped it on to her finger above her wedding ring. 'And there it will stay,' he told her. 'I should like you to wear it every day. The necklace, do you think?' He fastened it round her neck. 'These were my great-grandmother's—they have been handed down over the years, added to and altered. There are some rather fine sapphires too, but diamonds seem right with this dress. The bracelet, and the earrings—you will have to put these on yourself. Come to the mirror.'

Octavia fastened them and then stood looking at her reflection. The jewels scintillated back at her shown off to perfection by the soft pink of her gown. Lucas was standing behind her, looking at her in the mirror, and their eyes met. 'They're fabulous,' she told him. 'I don't know how to thank you. I—I don't suppose they get worn often.'

He answered her lazily. 'Oh, I shouldn't say that—there are a certain number of official functions I attend, and naturally you will come with me. But you will wear the ring, as I said, and there is a charming antique diamond brooch which is quite suitable for you to wear on your day dresses.' He came a step nearer. 'I like you with earrings, too.'

She turned to face him. 'Then I'll wear them every day—not these, of course, I'll look for something plain…'

'No need, there are some in the jewel box. I'll let you have it and you can choose whatever you wish from it.' He smiled slowly. 'You're beautiful, Octavia. I'm proud of you.'

A pleasant little glow warmed her insides. Lucas had always been kind and friendly and very understanding, but now there was something else—as though he didn't see her just as a suitable companion to run his home and care for his little daughter, but as a girl to whom he was attracted. It was a pity that there was no time to explore this interesting train of thought, because Berendina had found them and between excited appraisal of the diamonds and vivid descriptions of what Charlie had said and how Mrs Stubbs had re-tied her sash and Juffrouw Hinksma's approval of the new dress, there was no time to say anything else.

The guests began to arrive then, those Octavia had already met in Friesland, and they all went into dinner, and she was too busy being a good hostess to allow her thoughts to stray. And afterwards, when they had returned to the drawing room, Lucas's friends and more family began to arrive. The big room filled, while she stood beside Lucas in the doorway, being introduced and wished well by a bewildering number of people, most of whose names she had failed to remember, but all of whom, she thanked heaven, spoke English. They were on the point of leaving their place to stroll among their guests, when Marcus arrived. He shook Lucas's hand, gave Octavia an unexpected kiss, saying: 'I'm entitled to that—we're cousins now,' and then went on: 'I hope you will let Octavia come with me to the Kurhaus next week, Lucas—there's a splendid concert and I've two tickets for it.'

'Oh, I don't think...' began Octavia, to be interrupted by Lucas, very smooth, saying:

'Why not? I've a good deal of work to catch up on and shall be out most evenings. You will enjoy an evening out, Octavia.'

If he wanted to be rid of her, all right! She couldn't care less, she told herself, and accepted gracefully, and later in the evening she responded to Marcus's chatting-up with more warmth than she actually felt, out of sheer annoyance at Lucas's casual attitude.

The same strong feelings caused her to go out and buy a new dress for the occasion, a long-sleeved, high-necked silk jersey dress, eye-catching in its simplicity. It was a great pity that Lucas wasn't there to see her in it but he had telephoned to say that he wouldn't be home until late and she was to enjoy herself.

Marcus proved to be an amusing companion, lighthearted and flatteringly attentive, but Octavia found herself wishing the evening was over long before the concert was half finished. Perhaps because she didn't care for modern music, and the second half of the programme was given over entirely to that, she was quite relieved when the last clapping had died away and the audience began to leave, and when Marcus suggested that they should have a late supper in the restaurant she declined, pleading a quite mythical early morning engagement the next day. 'I enjoyed it,' she added mendaciously, and laughed helplessly when he gave her a droll look with the comment:

'More than I did—all that wailing and scraping—I don't pretend to understand modern music.' He added ingenuously, 'It was nice being with you, though; we must do it again, often.'

They were making their way towards his car, and Octavia stopped under a lamp post to give him a very direct look. 'Only if Lucas isn't free and—and doesn't mind.'

'Good lord, old Lucas never fusses about anything. It's a bit awkward sometimes, because one never quite knows what he's thinking. He's got a nasty temper, though, but you'll know about that.'

They were in the car driving back towards den Haag and she murmured something, glad that they hadn't far to go and there would be no need to carry on a long conversation. She wished him goodnight outside the house and felt guilty when Marcus said laughingly: 'No, I won't come in, thank you, and don't apologise for not asking me, Octavia.' He kissed her lightly on the cheek. 'Lucky Lucas!'

She had forgotten him by the time the great door closed behind her and she hadn't taken two steps into the hall before Daan appeared.

'*Mevrouw—Gelukkig…*' he switched to English. 'Mrs Stubbs—she is suddenly ill and I prepare to telephone the professor.'

'Where is he?' Octavia cast her wrap on to a chair and

started towards the small sitting room where there was a telephone.

'At the hospital, *mevrouw*—he telephoned a short time ago to ask if you had gone out.'

She wondered about that and then dismissed it. 'I'll go and see Mrs Stubbs, Daan, shall I? I might be able to discover if it's serious or not.'

She raced up the staircase, her skirts held high, and across the gallery and up another smaller flight to where the staff had their rooms.

Mrs Stubbs was lying in her bed, looking very ill and moaning from time to time. She stopped long enough to say: 'Bless you, Sister—it's me stomach.'

Octavia took hold of a damp clammy hand and felt a rapid pulse and cast an experienced eye over the greenish white of the patient's face. 'Have you been sick?' she wanted to know.

Mrs Stubbs nodded. 'Oh, I'ave, something chronic.'

'And the pain's here?' Octavia laid a gentle hand over the folds of Mrs Stubbs' voluminous nightgown.

'Something cruel. Am I going to die, Sister dear?'

Octavia smiled reassuringly. 'No, my dear. I may be wrong, but I rather think that you have appendicitis, and you know what we're going to do? Charlie and Daan will carry you downstairs and I'm going to drive you to hospital—the Professor is there and he'll see to things.'

Mrs Stubbs closed her eyes and sighed. 'Anything you say, Sister dear.'

Daan and Charlie and Juffrouw Hinksma were all very helpful. They got Mrs Stubbs downstairs very quietly so as not to wake the others, while Daan went and fetched the small Fiat which was kept in the garage for anyone to use and Octavia, her wrap cast round her shoulders, got into the driver's seat with Mrs Stubbs beside her. She hadn't driven in Holland yet, but at least she knew where the hospital was; she had made a point of seeking it out on one of her shopping expeditions, and there wasn't a great deal of traffic about. It might have been better to have called an ambulance, but it would have meant time lost while she talked to the ambulance station while someone translated—and perhaps she should have got a doctor—but who? She swung the little car into the forecourt of the hospital, told Mrs Stubbs to hang on for just a few more minutes and ran inside its vast entrance.

There was a young man crossing the hall as she went in and she accosted him without waste of time. 'Professor van der Weijnen,' she uttered urgently. 'I'm his wife…' She paused to ask: 'Do you understand English?'

'Certainly, *mevrouw*.' He smiled at her. 'I am happy to meet you. I am one of the junior anaesthetists and work under the Professor. You wish to see him?'

'It's urgent. Could someone tell him that I've brought Mrs Stubbs here, and that she's ill?'

'At once, *mevrouw*. You have her in a car? If you would wait with her…'

Mrs Stubbs was relieved to see her again. She was also in a good deal of pain. Octavia was holding her close, doing her best to comfort her, when the door opened and Lucas's bulk filled the opening.

Octavia's voice shook with relief. 'Lucas—I didn't know what to do, so I brought her here—Daan said…' She pulled herself together and said quietly: 'Abdominal pain, intermittent, fast pulse and sweating, vomited twice.'

A gleam came and went in Lucas's eyes, but he answered gravely. 'You did the right thing, my dear. There's a stretcher on the way—I'll get her looked at at once.' He leaned across her and took Mrs Stubbs's pulse and then stood aside as two porters came to take her inside. 'Are you going home,' he asked, 'or do you want to wait and see what's happening?'

'I'll wait, please.' She got out and went into the hospital with him, and halfway across the hall he stopped and looked at her.

'That's a very pretty dress. Is it new?'

His voice was so casual that she wanted to hurt him. 'Yes—I bought it specially for the concert this evening—if you remember, I went with Marcus.'

'Oh, I remembered,' he told her quietly. 'You'll excuse me if I go along to the surgical unit? There's a waiting room…'

She watched his great back disappearing down a corridor. He was almost out of sight when she realised that she was in love with him.

CHAPTER EIGHT

OCTAVIA dozed off after an hour. It was chilly in the waiting room, but she had drawn up a small hard chair to a radiator, kicked off her elegant slippers and with her stockinged feet on it and her wrap snug round her shoulders, she had closed her eyes the better to think. It was strange, now that she had come to think about it, that she hadn't realised that she loved Lucas, but really there was nothing to do about it. It would make life very difficult, she could see that, having to pretend for ever and ever that her feelings for him were no deeper than friendship, for she could see little chance of him falling in love with her—indeed, it had seemed to her lately that he was avoiding her, and what newly married man would actually suggest that his wife should spend an evening with another man, even if it were his cousin? It would have been wonderful to have had her father to talk to… She blinked back tears and decided that sleep, for the moment at any rate, was the best way out of her problems.

She was wakened by Lucas's voice, saying something with some vehemence in his own language, and she sat up at once, forgetful of the tear stains on her cheeks. 'So sorry,' she said apologetically, and felt her heart rocket at the sight of him. 'I dozed off.' She started scrabbling around for her slippers and saw that he was holding them.

'My feet...they're new—the slippers, and the radiator's warm. Is Mrs Stubbs all right? Have they operated?'

'Yes, she's in bed. Would you like to see her?'

He held out the slippers and she put them on. 'Oh, yes, please. Is it allowed? I mean, it must be very late.'

He looked a lot younger when he smiled; he should smile more, she thought lovingly. 'Early—it's half past two in the morning.'

'Daan,' she exclaimed, 'and Juffrouw Hinksma, they'll be waiting—and poor old Charlie...'

'I telephoned them half an hour ago. I told them to go to bed.' He took her wrap and put it over her shoulders and she went with him out of the room and along a passage to a lift. As they travelled upwards she said anxiously: 'You're not annoyed that I came here? I didn't know any doctors and I was afraid that the ambulance people might not understand—I don't even know if I can call an ambulance...'

The lift stopped and he opened the doors. 'I've been very neglectful of you. We must have an hour together some time and I'll fill you in.' He had crossed a wide corridor and pushed open swing doors and Octavia slipped past him into a foyer with corridors leading from it. 'Come this way.'

Mrs Stubbs was in a small ward, lying very still in bed with her eyes shut but she opened them as Octavia got to the bedside.

'Sister dear, what are they going to do?' She looked puzzled. 'And how did I get here?'

'It's done, Mrs Stubbs, and you're fine again. You're in bed in the Professor's hospital, so you'll be quite all right. I'll come and see you each day, but now you're going to have a nice sleep.'

The blue eyes lighted on the Professor's large form at

the end of the bed. 'Ain't I lucky?' remarked Mrs Stubbs, and dozed off.

'She'll do very well,' remarked Lucas as they sat drinking coffee in Night Sister's office. 'A nasty appendix, though.' He put his cup down. 'I'll be in tomorrow, Zuster Woulters. Shall we go home, my dear?'

In the Rolls, driving smoothly through the deserted streets, he asked: 'How did you get on in the Fiat?'

'Well, I was a little scared and I haven't got a licence here either, only I didn't think of that.' Octavia gave a gasp. 'The Fiat—I've left it in front of the hospital!'

'I asked a porter to run it round to the Consultants' park—someone can bring it back tomorrow. Better not drive yourself until we've seen to that licence. Which sort of car do you like to drive?'

He had drawn up before the house but had made no attempt to get out.

'Me? I've no idea. We had a very old Morris, but I don't need a car. I like walking and there are always buses or taxis.'

He said blandly: 'But a car is useful—you would be able to take Berendina out. In the summer that would be rather nice, don't you think? I'll have a look round.'

Her 'Very well,' was meek. Of course she would be expected to live up to his status. If she didn't drive her own car, people might say that he was mean. She dismissed the thought as completely unworthy; there wasn't a spark of meanness in him.

They went into the house together, but Lucas left her at the foot of the staircase, saying that he had some reading to do.

'But it's gone three o'clock,' she expostulated. 'You'll be tired...'

'I'll do well enough. Go to bed yourself, Octavia, and

thank you for acting so quickly this evening. I'm very fond of our Mrs Stubbs; we must get her well again as soon as we can.'

She paused on the bottom step, reluctant to leave him. 'Could she not come back here? I could nurse her.'

'That would be an excellent idea—I'll see about it. Do you wish to see her tomorrow?'

'Please. When's the best time?'

'I have patients at my rooms in the morning, but I shall go to the hospital first, there are a couple of cases I want to check on. I'll come for you about ten o'clock—a little sooner—take you to the hospital and call for you when I've finished with my patients—about midday, I should think. You won't want to stay with Mrs Stubbs all that time, but you can sit in Sister's office or wait in the Consultants' room.'

'Thank you. Where are your rooms?'

'Quite close by—you shall see them tomorrow. Now go to bed.' He sounded suddenly irritable so that her good-night was subdued, and she ran upstairs as fast as she could and didn't look back.

There was no sign of irritability at breakfast a few hours later. Octavia, coming downstairs promptly although it had cost her an effort to get out of bed, her beautiful face pale from too little sleep, was peeved to see that Lucas looked exactly as he always did; calm, well-shaven, impeccably dressed, his blue eyes as bright and alert as if he had had eight hours' sleep instead of barely three. What was more, he dealt patiently with Berendina's countless questions, remarking to Octavia, that he had already been to the kitchen to tell everyone that Mrs Stubbs was operated upon and safely in her bed at the hospital. 'They will all wish to see her,' he went on. 'Perhaps you could arrange that? Two at a time, I should think, spread over the next few days. You will be able to go when you like, of course.'

Because she was a senior consultant's wife. She wished that she knew more about his work. A wish, she thought unhappily, that she had a dozen times a day and would probably continue to have for the rest of her days. And hard on the thought Lucas observed: 'Perhaps you would like to see my rooms? We might call in on my way back from the hospital after I have fetched you.'

Her pale face was tinted a delicate pink. 'Oh, I'd like that very much, Lucas.' She looked so excited that he laughed.

'What an enthusiastic girl you are! On the *Socrates*...' He didn't finish what he was saying, which disappointed her, and his manner, which had been almost lighthearted, became blandly pleasant. It remained so when Daan came into the room to tell her that Mijnheer Marcus wanted to speak to her on the telephone.

He wanted to know if she would go to the Mauritshuis, a seventeenth-century mansion with a magnificent collection of Old Masters, that morning. 'Old Lucas won't have the time,' he told her lightly, 'and you couldn't possibly go alone.'

She told him about Mrs Stubbs, said: 'Another time, perhaps,' and went back to the breakfast room. It was Berendina who wanted to know what her uncle Marcus had wanted; Lucas was deep in a sheaf of typewritten notes. Octavia kept her eyes on the top of his head while she explained to the little girl and saw him give an irritable shake to the papers and then lower them. 'My dear Octavia,' he said smoothly, 'why don't you go? Marcus is such good company—just the man to show you round.'

She looked rather defiantly at him across the table. 'But I'm going to see Mrs Stubbs—she's much more important.

Besides, you've just said that you'll take me to your rooms afterwards.'

His smile was thin. 'Hardly to be compared with the Mauritshuis.'

She folded her napkin and rolled it into its silver ring. 'I'll be the best judge of that,' she told him austerely.

She was waiting for him when he came to fetch her at ten o'clock, and because she was his wife and he was an important man at the hospital, she had taken care with her clothes: the grey suit with a soft cashmere sweater under it and a perky little velvet hat. She was wearing her new shoes too, brown calf and expensive to go with the handbag and gloves she had already bought. She was glad she had taken so much trouble when Lucas saw her, for his look was approving, although he said nothing. Only as they got into the car, she asked timidly: 'Do I look—well, staid enough?'

'Hardly that, but quite charming. Do you feel that you should dress to—er—compliment a middle-aged husband?'

A little rush of temper almost took her breath. 'Oh, don't keep harping on your age!' she snapped. 'You're not even middle-aged—why do you keep reminding me—and yourself—about it?'

Lucas eased the Rolls between the hospital entrance gateposts. 'Perhaps because the difference in our ages is rather great,' his voice was silky. 'Besides, I have been married before.'

Octavia choked and then said with spirit, 'Oh, am I such a failure? I—I thought—I was beginning to think…' She had no chance to finish the incoherent flow of words her muddled thinking had produced. They had arrived, and a posse of white-coated young men were advancing upon them. Lucas leaned out to speak to one of them and her door was opened and she was whisked away without even a goodbye. Perhaps, she thought gloomily as she was escorted to the lift, he'll not come for me, perhaps he's so angry he'll forget, and perhaps that would be just as well—for she had been on the point of saying a great many unsuitable things. It would never do to let him see that she was in love with him. Life, already complicated, would be even more so.

Mrs Stubbs was awake, sitting up against her pillows looking washed-out but determinedly getting better. She accepted the flowers Octavia had brought with her, listened to the various messages from members of the household and informed Octavia that on the whole the hospital, although foreign, wasn't too bad. 'A nice enough young woman, the Sister,' she pronounced in a rather wispy voice, 'though I'd rather you was 'ere, Sister dear.'

'Well, I am,' Octavia pointed out, 'and I shall come each day, you know, and all the others are coming to see you too, one or two at a time, and as soon as you're well enough, the Professor says you are to come home. I'll look after you and you'll be on your feet again in no time, though you're not to do anything for quite a while.'

'I can baby-sit,' said Mrs Stubbs stoutly, 'when you and the Professor goes out of an evening. I'm not one to take someone's vittles and not pay for 'em.'

Octavia agreed hurriedly. Mrs Stubbs had her pride; when she got home she would see Juffrouw Hinksma and ask her to save up all the mending and let the vast array of copper pans in the kitchen go unpolished so that her assistant would have plenty to do during her convalescence.

She stayed with Mrs Stubbs until the ward Sister came along and invited her to have coffee in her office while the patient was examined by the Surgical Registrar and generally put to rights by the nurses. 'And I'm ter sit out termorrow, Sister dear,' she told Octavia when she had settled herself once more by the bed. 'I'll be 'ome in no time.'

Octavia smiled and nodded and murmured agreement, struck by the thought that Mrs Stubbs had taken to living in the lovely old house in den Haag with all the ease in the world. So had Charlie, for that matter. It was already home to them, and so was it her home now. She thought with a touch of sadness of her home in Alresford; Lucas had said that they would go back there and decide what to do with it, and she supposed she would take his advice when the time came, but already she was aware of the magic of the Dutch home. She would be content to live there for the rest of her life—that was, if Lucas would be content to have her. She wasn't quite sure about that.

She was fetched very politely by a young and scared-looking medical student, so that when she had taken her leave of Mrs Stubbs she set herself to put him at his ease. 'I can't speak Dutch,' she told him chattily, 'at least, only a very little, so you must air your English—it's very good.'

He looked pleased. 'The Professor sent me, *mevrouw*, because my English is quite good and he wishes you not to be puzzled…'

'Oh, good. Tell me, how long have you been studying? When do you take your exams?'

She listened to his eager, halting English, stoking it gently with more questions. By the time they had reached the front hall, not hurrying, they were on excellent terms, although the young man froze at the sight of Lucas, waiting there for them. He looked at them, faintly amused, and the boy went an unhappy scarlet; Octavia didn't know why, but she had to go to his rescue. She said: 'Hullo, Lucas,' in a bright social sort of voice. 'How nice to be fetched by someone who speaks such super English! I should have been lost…' She held out a hand. 'I don't know your name, do I?'

'De Wesselijs, *mevrouw*, Piet.'

'Well, goodbye, Piet. I expect we'll see each other again some time.'

'Oh, I do hope so, *mevrouw*.' He cast a nervous glance at Lucas and rushed ahead to open the door for them and was gravely thanked by the Professor, who then closed his mouth firmly until they were in the car.

'You appear to have quite an effect on my students, Octavia.'

She looked at him, round-eyed. 'Me? But I only saw one of them—such a nice boy, too.' She frowned. 'And if it comes to that you seem to have quite an effect on them too, if his red face was anything to judge by.'

Lucas had turned the car into the street, thick with midday traffic. He said mildly: 'I try to teach them. There was a good deal of competition as to who should fetch you—you see, they had seen you earlier this morning.'

Octavia went pink. 'Oh.' She added tartly: 'Well, you could have solved that by coming for me yourself.' She was sorry the moment she had spoken, she had sounded like a shrew, but apparently he hadn't noticed, for his:

'But my dear, why should I deprive them of that pleasure?' was uttered with casual good nature.

It was just the kind of remark he would make, she thought savagely; she could take it seriously or not. Not, she decided.

Lucas's rooms were in a quiet backwater of a street, lined with tall, thin houses, their important front doors adorned with discreet brass plates. 'A Dutch Harley Street,' said Octavia out loud.

'You might call it that,' Lucas agreed, 'although there is a fair sprinkling of solicitors and barristers and so on, as well as the odd embassy.' He stopped smoothly half way down the street, helped her out and ushered her through an elaborately carved doorway and up a short staircase. He had the whole of the first floor, waiting room, office for his receptionist; a large, placid girl with a soft voice, a small surgery behind it with a nurse sitting at a small desk, writing; a middle-aged woman this time with a rather vinegary face which changed surprisingly when she smiled, and at the end of the waiting room, his consulting room, comfortable in a severe way with a large desk and a wall covered with book shelves crammed to overflowing.

Octavia stood in the middle of the grey carpet and looked around her. 'It's absurd,' she told him, 'I'm not even sure just what you are. You're the senior consultant anaesthetist at the hospital, but do you have a general practice too? And is it private or whatever you call the National Health?'

He was leaning against the desk, staring at her. 'Both. I would have told you, but I wasn't sure if you would be interested. Are you interested, Octavia?'

She looked away from him. 'Yes, of course. I've been wrapped up in myself, haven't I? I'm sorry… I'm getting over Father a little, I have to, and I'm very happy, you know. I love Berendina and everyone is so kind…'

'And I? Have I been kind?'

'Oh, Lucas, yes—you made everything so easy and you've given me so much.' She added in a mumbling voice, 'I wish I saw more of you, though.'

He put his hands in his pockets, his gaze steady. 'You are, for the moment, very vulnerable, Octavia. One phase of your life has come to an end and you have only just embarked on another, a dangerous period when you might make the wrong decision.'

She couldn't understand him at all. 'I don't think I quite…' she began, and was very surprised when he asked:

'Do you like young Marcus?'

'Well, yes.' She looked at him enquiringly. 'Why do you ask? You asked before…' She drew a deep breath. 'Lucas, are you always so busy? I mean, don't you ever take a day off or—or come home more often for tea or—or anything?' And before he could answer: 'That's the silliest question a doctor's wife could ask, isn't it? Don't answer.'

'No, I'm not going to—not now, at any rate.' He smiled a little. 'You're such a pretty girl, Octavia.'

'Thank you.' She said it quietly although her heart had given a great leap, to flop back again almost at once. What was the use of a pretty face if he didn't love it? 'I hope I'm being a good wife—the kind you wanted—I'll get better.'

His face was inscrutable. 'You're a very good wife, my dear, but not what I expected. No, don't look like that; what I meant to say was that I didn't realise at the time…' The telephone's shrill ringing brought him to a halt and Octavia, listening eagerly, could have flung the wretched thing to the ground. The conversation was brief, but when Lucas put the receiver back he made no attempt to finish what he had been going to say, and when she prompted him he laughed and shook his head. 'Saved by the bell,' he observed. 'Shall we go?'

He was charming on the short drive back to the house, but once there he only stopped long enough to receive the hug which Berendina—brought home from school by Charlie—bestowed upon him. 'I'll be late this evening,' he told Octavia with a pleasant coolness which prevented her asking why.

'I'll put dinner back,' she suggested.

'Don't bother, I'll get a meal there. It's unlikely that I'll be home before midnight or later. Have a pleasant evening.'

She said very evenly: 'I've started on a set of tapestry chair covers. They'll keep me occupied.' Like those mediaeval ladies who spent their lives stitching tapestries, she thought despondently, and then chided herself for wallowing in self-pity.

But she didn't set a single stitch that evening after her solitary dinner, but just sat staring at the canvas on its frame, quite unable to follow the pattern because she was crying so hard.

She was ripe for Marcus's telephone call the next morning. Lucas, it seemed, on enquiry from Charlie, had breakfasted very early, and Daan offered the further information that he had a busy day at the hospital. Octavia, refusing the offer of a nice boiled egg with her breakfast, sat down to supervise her small stepdaughter, drank a great many cups of coffee and took her to school. She walked back home rather aimlessly. She could of course do the flowers, or she could telephone the retired schoolmaster whom Lucas had asked to give her Dutch lessons, leaving her to decide which days and at what time. Perhaps it would be a good idea, she reflected as she went indoors, if she telephoned at once. Lessons would keep her busy and take her mind off Lucas.

She was actually reaching for the instrument when it rang, and when she answered it, Marcus's cheerful voice wished her a good morning and wanted to know if she were busy.

She said, 'No,' so promptly that he wasted no time. 'Good—let's go for a brisk walk by the sea, and I've got tickets for the ballet this evening. No, don't say no—you can let me know later on in the day if Lucas is going to be late. I'll be at your place in fifteen minutes.'

It would be nice to be with someone who cheered her up and kept her thoughts from straying to her own troubles. Octavia fetched her new raincoat because it was a blustery, damp morning, tied a scarf over her hair, and went to find Juffrouw Hinksma who was going to see Mrs Stubbs that morning. She managed to say, 'I go this afternoon,' quite adequately, and the housekeeper nodded with approval, rattling off a few cheerful remarks which Octavia couldn't understand at all. Not that it mattered, as long as Mrs Stubbs got her message. She was conscious of Daan's disapproval when she told him that she was going to Scheveningen with Mijnheer Marcus, and added hastily: 'But only for a short while—I'll be back in good time to fetch Berendina.'

Marcus was in tearing spirits and the walk was a success. He parked the car at the Kurhaus and they had coffee before setting out in the teeth of a now howling wind, and Octavia, grateful for his arm to keep her on her feet, wished that it was Lucas who was with her and not Marcus.

She shouted into the wind: 'Marcus, what do you do? For a living, I mean?'

He roared with laughter. 'Nothing, dear girl. I look after my property and play polo and go skiing in the winter and sail quite a bit in the summer,' and when she looked at him in astonishment, 'Lucas could do the same, you know. He's got masses of money, but he chooses to work at the hospital—for nothing, mind you, and he's helped more lame dogs over stiles than I have hairs on my head. A good chap, old Lucas.'

'He's not old!' Octavia bellowed above the wind.

Marcus gave her a sideways look. 'No, of course not, dear girl, just a figure of speech. The family hold him in great esteem, though he can lash out if he's a mind to. He's got the nasty van der Weijnen temper.' He added slyly: 'But I don't suppose you've come up against that.'

Octavia muttered that she hadn't, which wasn't quite true, but really Lucas's temper was a small matter. When you loved someone their shortcomings somehow didn't signify.

There was a telephone message when she got home—Lucas thought it unlikely that he would be home until very late in the evening. She took Berendina to school and telephoned Marcus. 'Lucas can't get home until late,' she told him brightly, 'so I'd love to come this evening. Is it a dressy occasion?'

'Splendid. Yes—wear something dazzling, although you're always that.'

She had an early dinner, prudently refusing to dine with Marcus, just in case Lucas should arrive home early after all. But he didn't, and with Berendina tucked up in bed, and Juffrouw Hinksma warned to keep an eye on her, Octavia went downstairs. She had decided to wear the green silk jersey. Her diamond ring was always on her finger, so she had complemented it with the earrings, picked up the dark brown velvet cloak she had bought herself and arrived in the hall just as Marcus was admitted. They were still exchanging lighthearted greetings when the door opened again and Lucas came in.

He shut the door behind him before he said anything. 'Octavia,' his voice was gentle, 'I didn't know you were going out.' He looked across to Marcus, his brows lifted. 'With Marcus?'

'I was,' said Octavia instantly, 'but now you're home, I'm not. You sent a message to say you'd be very late.'

'Indeed I did. The lecture I was to give has been postponed; I don't need to go to Utrecht, after all.' He added on a note of polite enquiry: 'Where are you two going?'

'The ballet. But we're not…'

He gave her one of his kind smiles. 'Why not? I've a mass of work to get through.'

'Have you had dinner?'

'Something on a tray. Daan will look after me.' He turned to Marcus. 'How's life, Marcus, any plans for winter sports?'

The two men talked for a few minutes and Octavia, wanting something to do, went over to where Lucas had thrown his coat down. As she picked it up and folded it tidily to lay over a chair, something fell out of one of the pockets. Two tickets for the concert to be given by the Amsterdam Concertgebouw Orchestra in the Circus theatre in Scheveningen. Octavia turned round with them in her hand, her mouth open to speak, but she was given no chance. Lucas had reached her side, taken them from her, torn them deliberately in two and thrown them in the wastepaper basket.

'You'll be late,' he observed, even more gently than before.

Octavia watched the ballet with unseeing eyes, turning over in her mind the two possibilities the tickets in Lucas's coat conjured up. Had they been for her and him, or for him and someone else? He could so easily have told her that he would have to go out again that evening; he so often did, and she had never questioned it, but now she did, to the exclusion of everything else.

'You'd like to go straight home, I expect?' Marcus asked as they left the theatre, not even bothering to ask her to have supper with him. And when she nodded, he put her in the car and climbed in beside her. As they went back along the Scheveningse Weg he said in a cheerful, matter-of-fact voice: 'Spoilt your evening, didn't I? Sorry about that: I like you very much, my dear, much too much to make you unhappy. I've a feeling that Lucas wasn't best pleased to see me this evening. Of course he's in love—for the first time, because you can't count his first marriage—and he wants you all to himself. It's not much use telling him we're just good friends, and that's all we are. Would you like me to make myself scarce for a while?'

'Yes, please,' said Octavia while she digested the bit about Lucas being in love. He wasn't, of course…

'I'm coming in,' said Marcus as they stopped outside Lucas's house.

It wasn't late. Daan opened the door to them and Lucas came out of his study as they stood in the hall. He enquired pleasantly as to the ballet, expressed the view that it wasn't every man's meat and asked Marcus to stay for a drink.

Marcus declined and presently bade them goodnight and left the house. He had barely got the other side of the door when Octavia asked urgently: 'Lucas, those tickets—were they for us—I mean, you and me?'

He strolled into the drawing room and she followed him and watched him go over to the drinks tray. 'Would you like a drink?' he asked, and when she shook her head, poured himself a whisky. 'Is it important?' he wanted to know.

'Yes—yes, it is. I wouldn't have gone with Marcus…'

He turned to face her. 'My dear Octavia,' his voice was bland, 'I hope you don't regard me as some kind of mid-Victorian husband who allows his wife no freedom. I'm delighted that you enjoyed yourself.'

She longed to tell him that she hadn't, but bit the words back. She suspected that behind the blandness was a nasty temper waiting for an excuse to pop out. She murmured nothing in particular, added that she was tired and wished him goodnight. In her bedroom it struck her that he hadn't told her for whom the tickets had been.

She had to admit that she missed Marcus's cheerful company during the next few days, but only because he had helped to pass them for her. Now she plunged into Dutch lessons, spending hours reciting impossible sounding words and trying them out on Daan and Juffrouw Hinksma and the housemaids, and when she was worn out with that, plying her needle with all the concentrated energy of someone on piece work. The one great drawback was that it allowed her to think, and the only thing she thought about was Lucas.

She became a little wan during the next week. The effort of maintaining an unflurried front towards him was wearing her out. It was lucky that she had Berendina to love, and at the end of the week she had Mrs Stubbs to look after—a rather thin Mrs Stubbs but already demanding that she be given something to do. She tut-tutted with pleased disapproval over the unpolished saucepans and then set herself to mend, with fairylike stitches, a tear in one of Lucas's shirts. And when she could be persuaded to sit back and rest for an hour or two it was Charlie who came to sit with her, entertaining her with tales of former employers and reading her extracts from the *Daily Mirror*, which the Professor had ordered specially for them, in his cheerful Cockney voice. Octavia, coming upon them enjoying each other's company so contentedly, told Lucas over dinner that evening that it did her good just to look at them.

'You have no idea how happy you've made them,' she told him. 'Just think, if you hadn't been at the hospital just when they came in, you might never have met them and given them a home.'

He paused in the buttering of a roll. 'That applies to us too, Octavia.'

She blushed under his eye, not quite knowing what to say, and then made haste to change the conversation. 'It's a pity Berendina was asleep when you came home,' she observed. 'She's had an invitation to her friend Lisa's party—it's her birthday Thursday and there's no school in the afternoon. It's to start at two o'clock. She asked me to let you see the invitation if she didn't see you herself.'

'Lisa Hoffmann? Yes, of course she can go, they're good friends of ours. Are they going to fetch her?'

'Well, no. I wondered if I could drive her. I've got my licence now and I'll be careful.' She added: 'It's only Leiden.'

Lucas didn't answer at once. 'Take the Fiat, but I should like you to come back before the evening rush starts. If you leave there not later than half past four, you should be home before it starts.'

'All right, I promise I'll do that. Mevrouw Hoffmann asked me if I'd have tea with her while the party's on and I'll leave punctually.'

He nodded, 'By the way, I don't seem to have seen anything of Marcus lately.' The statement was really a question.

Octavia tried to keep her voice matter-of-fact. 'No—well, nor have I—perhaps he's away somewhere. It must be a bit boring not having a job.'

Lucas gave her a considered glance. 'I should have thought so, although I imagine he enjoys life—he's a great sportsman, you know.'

'Yes.' She took some fish from the platter Daan was holding. 'Should Berendina take a present with her?'

The gleam in Lucas's eyes might have been amusement or irritation. 'Oh, certainly. Has she enough pocket money to buy it?'

Octavia grinned. 'Lord no—she saw something she wants to give you for Christmas and she spent all her money on that, but don't let her know I told you, will you?'

'No, I shan't do that—but Christmas is months away.'

'About eight weeks.' She looked up and saw his frown. 'Don't you like Christmas?'

'It has been the custom for many years to have all the family here for Christmas Day and quite a number of them stay for a few days.'

'That will be fun—All the people who came to the reception?'

'A good half of them.'

'And will you be home? I mean, not working late or going early or anything like that.'

He said smoothly: 'It depends, Octavia. Why do you want to know?'

She looked at him in astonishment. 'Well, of course I want to know! It wouldn't be…' She stopped, aware that she had been on the point of telling him that Christmas wouldn't be Christmas without him. And now she came to study his face, he was mocking her.

'I'll do my best to give you exact details of my whereabouts,' he told her.

It was a dull, cold day when Octavia left the house with Berendina. It was only seventeen kilometres to Leiden going by the motorway. She drove the Fiat out of the city and joined the stream of traffic heading north, not nervous once she was actually in the driver's seat. Berendina, in a party dress and a thick coat with a hood, chattered away non-stop, sometimes in English, sometimes in Dutch, and Octavia painstakingly tried to answer her in her own language, something which the little girl found shatteringly funny so that they arrived at Mevrouw Hoffmann's house in high spirits. Here they parted company, Berendina to join her small friends in an upstairs play room while Octavia found herself with half a dozen other youngish women in Mevrouw Hoffmann's drawing room, an imposing apartment furnished with unlikely gilt chairs, a great many cushions and some enormous gloomy pictures upon its walls.

Octavia, looking surreptitiously around her, felt quite weighed down. She was even more weighed down by the young matrons in the room. They were friendly enough but far too curious; besides, from time to time they made oblique references to Margriet. Octavia wished that her Dutch was good enough to be certain that she understood every word they were saying and not just a few here and there, or so bad that she wouldn't have been bothered. She sipped her weak, milkless tea and nibbled little biscuits and made conversation, avoiding most of the more searching questions by pretending that she couldn't understand a word the speaker was saying.

It was a relief when the hideous porcelain clock on the table beside her chimed half past four and she could make her excuses and leave. It took a few minutes to prise Berendina away from her friends and for them both to say their goodbyes. They were, indeed, in the middle of these when the front door bell was pealed and Marcus, of all people, was admitted.

He looked as surprised as Octavia did and a little awkward too. 'I thought you'd gone away,' she said, aware of the awkwardness and wondering why, and then finding the answer almost immediately. Not all the young matrons were matrons; a big sister had brought one of the small guests, a pretty girl with fair hair worn loose on her shoulders and wearing the swirling layers of shirts and sweaters and topcoats which Octavia had seen in the fashion magazines and decided weren't quite her. Marcus gravitated to her side as though drawn by a magnet, murmured something to make her smile and then came back to Octavia.

'You've met her? Isn't she quite something? It wasn't until I saw you and old Lucas together at the reception that

I realised that being married might be quite fun. Iona's known me for years, but she thought I was too idle rich.' He grinned engagingly. 'She's promised to consider me if I'll get a job. I can't do anything, but old Lucas will help—he always does.' He added with unflattering anxiety: 'I say, do you want to be driven back?'

Octavia giggled. 'No, thanks. I've got the Fiat, only I have to get home before the rush hour.' Her eyes caught sight of the clock on the wall behind him and she uttered a small shriek. 'It's five o'clock! I'll never be back...' She looked around. 'Where's Berendina?'

'You stay there, I'll get her—and don't worry, there's plenty of time and an easy run back.'

All the same it was another five minutes before Octavia had made her final farewells and hurried Berendina out to where the Fiat was parked in the drive. The afternoon had darkened and the sky had a curious woolly look which Octavia didn't much fancy, and as well as that, by the time she had made her way through Leiden's streets and joined the motorway, the traffic was building up fast.

It was when they were almost on the outskirts of den Haag that Octavia noticed the wisps of fog creeping ahead of them. The motorway was full of homegoing traffic now as well as great juggernauts making their fast journeys from one end of the country to the other, and the sky had become curiously low and grim.

'It's snowing!' exclaimed Berendina excitedly, only it wasn't snow, it was icy rain, freezing as it fell, settling on the windscreen with terrifying speed, so that the wipers lost their battle within seconds. Octavia slowed gradually, feeling the road surface glassy under the wheels, and moved cautiously and with her heart in her mouth, expecting to skid at any moment, into the slow lane. If it got much worse she would have to stop on the hard shoulder and wait until it cleared or the road was sanded. Traffic, swollen now by commuters, was streaming along the fast lane, apparently undeterred by the icy conditions, and just for a moment she was tempted to rejoin them; they were so near home. She was a good driver and not easily scared, but she had Berendina with her and she daren't risk it. Better to stay where she was, crawling towards the exit which would lead her into the city, for the motorway was already bypassing the suburbs.

But she had reckoned without the fog; suddenly it was all around them like a wet, stifling blanket. No breath of wind stirred it, only the icy rain fell steadily. Octavia dared not stop now; there had been a car on her tail and others behind it and if the transport lorry in front of her stopped, she would be lucky to escape with nothing more than a bump. As she realised this there was a sickening crash somewhere ahead of them, followed by a series of sinister grindings and clashes. The squeal of hydraulic brakes warned her that the huge vehicle ahead of her was slowing to a halt and she braked gently herself, praying that the driver behind wouldn't go into her. The visibility was now almost nil, it was inevitable that he should; she felt the car behind just touch the rear bumpers and thanked heaven that it was no worse. If they could stay as they were, there was a chance that no more damage would be done.

She switched off the engine and put a comforting arm round Berendina's small shoulders and the little girl buried her head against her coat. 'I don't like it,' she wailed. 'I want to go home, I'm frightened!'

Octavia kissed the flaxen head. 'Well, I don't really like it very much either, darling, but it won't last long, you know. We'll just stay here until the fog goes away and then we'll be home in no time—we're almost there anyway.'

'I want Papa,' declared Berendina, a wish silently

echoed by Octavia. She wasn't exactly afraid, but if Lucas had been with them, she could have left everything to him; he would have known what to do and when to do it. At the back of her mind was the uncomfortable doubt that conditions, instead of improving, might get worse. There was a good deal of noise now, distant shouts, and the almost continuous squeal of brakes—drivers coming along too fast despite the iced-up roads and no visibility at all, and the more prudent ones, finding themselves caught up in a tangle of fog-bound traffic—and far ahead of them an ominous glow. There would be utter chaos at the head of the queue, but at least they were comparatively safe where they were.

The comforting thought was snapped like a thread as the car behind caterpaulted into the Fiat, shattering the rear window, showering glass all over the back seat and doing heaven knew what damage. Octavia flung forward in her seat belt, instinctively flung her other arm round her small companion and although they fell sprawling together they were neither of them hurt. She helped the child back on to the seat and soothed her in a rather shaky voice while she tried to decide what was best to be done. At any moment some hefty transport might crash into them, sending the cars behind her into a tangled mass, buckling them hopelessly together, but if they got out of the car and tried to get off the hard shoulder into the fields beyond, they might easily fall on the slippery road. Besides, she had heard somewhere or other that one tended to walk in circles in a fog.

She fought a sick longing for Lucas, wishing for some miracle which would send him to them. Probably he would have no idea what had happened, although by now surely the whole hospital service would have been alerted; there must have been casualties up in front where the most damage had been done. If only she had left on time as Lucas had told her to, they would have been home…

Berendina's sobs gave way to an unhappy snivelling and Octavia hugged her close. It was cold with the rear window in shreds, letting in the icy fog and rain. It let in the shouts and cries and the distant crashing of cars still colliding, too.

They had been huddled together for what seemed a lifetime when Octavia, pausing in the telling of some hastily thought-up story to distract Berendina, heard a whistle, and shot up in her seat. 'Lucas!' she squealed. 'That's his whistle—when he calls Whiskey. He's here, Berendina, listen!'

The whistle came again and Octavia whistled in reply and then shouted from the open window, but the next time it came, the whistle was further away; he'd missed them. 'He's got to come back,' she told no one in particular, filled her lungs with fog and shouted again and for good measure, whistled too, but the noise was almost non-stop around them now. She doubted if he would hear her and there was no answer. All the same she took a deep breath again and bellowed 'Lucas!' at the top of her voice.

'No need to deafen me, my dear,' said Lucas, inches from her distraught head thrust through the window. He came a step nearer so that she could see him now, bent suddenly and kissed her half-opened mouth with swift urgency, pushed her gently back into her seat and leaned across to tweak his small daughter's hair. 'What a mercy that you can whistle,' he remarked cheerfully, and when they both broke into a babble of questions: 'Not now, my dears—I think we'd best get out of this as quickly as we can.'

Which they did, one each side of him, slipping and sliding as he led them across the short stretch of road and into the open fields beyond.

Once there, Octavia asked: 'Aren't we lost?'

'Not a bit of it. All we have to do is to keep that' and she knew he meant the fire ahead of them— 'on our right and walk across the field until we hit the lane on the other side. The car's there.'

She longed to ask how he had known that they were there, how he had reached them, but he had said not now. She held his hand tightly and trudged along, stumbling now and then, listening to his calm voice talking to Berendina on the other side of him, confident that they were quite safe now.

As they were. The lane was exactly where Lucas had said it would be, and there, miraculously was the Rolls. He bundled them in gently, wrapped them up in soft rugs and drove them home. It took ages, of course; the Rolls tiptoeing forward foot by foot into the dark nothingness in front of them until Lucas eased her gently to a halt before his own front door.

The pavement was like a skating rink. He carried Berendina in and then came back to help Octavia, who slid around in a clumsy fashion until he picked her up too and carried her up the steps. Her mumbled, 'So sorry,' was lost in the thickness of his sheepskin jacket.

The hall was a blaze of light with everyone there asking questions, offering advice and help. Lucas shed his jacket. 'A hot bath and dressing gown for you, Berendina. Perhaps Sasje will go with you—you can stay up for dinner. Octavia, come and sit down by the fire—a drink will do you good.' He smiled around at them all. 'Thank you all for your help—we'll have dinner a little earlier if we may so that Berendina can get to bed.'

He took Octavia's arm and led her to the small sitting room and sat her down by the fire. Someone had taken her coat and now he took the scarf from her shoulders and unzipped her boots and pulled them off. Only when she was sitting relaxed against the cushions with a loathed glass of whisky in her hand did Lucas sit opposite her and ask in a quiet voice: 'Tell me what happened, my dear.'

CHAPTER NINE

THERE was no reason why Lucas's placid face and even more placid voice should make her feel so guilty. She went red in the face even though she returned his intent gaze steadfastly.

'We—I left the Hoffmanns' half an hour late—no, it was nearer forty minutes by the time we got away.' She waited to see if he was going to say anything and when he didn't, she went on: 'I didn't forget. We were all ready to go—a bit late already because of so many people being there—and then I—I got held up.'

Lucas asked casually: 'Was Marcus there?'

'Yes—at least, he arrived just as we were going—that's why we left late.' She added miserably: 'I'm awfully sorry, I just didn't notice the time.'

He smiled at her, not at all nicely. 'Naturally not.' He went on harshly: 'You might have been killed, the pair of you—do you realise how dangerous it was?' The icy rage in his voice made her shiver. 'You should have thought of Berendina; one has to make certain sacrifices where children are concerned—it was one thing to risk your own life, but quite another to put hers at risk too, not to mention her fright.'

Octavia put her untouched drink down and got to her

stockinged feet. 'You make it sound as though I did it deliberately!'

He stared at her from his great chair. 'Not deliberately, but one's emotions sometimes get the better of one's good sense.'

She was suddenly furious with him, and hurt and disappointed as well. 'And a good thing too,' she said loudly. 'I'd rather let my emotions show than be half dead and—and dreary and reading sheaves of papers all the time and never going anywhere!'

She went from the room at a great rate because at any moment now she was going to burst into tears—a luxury she allowed herself when she reached her own room. They weren't tears of rage; she was crying because Lucas had kissed her as though he had wanted to, and he hadn't.

She went down to dinner presently, very well turned out in a wool dress, her shining hair hanging round her shoulders, her nicely made up face showing no trace of the tears she had shed. She had sent Berendina down first on the pretext that she wasn't ready, so that when she reached the drawing room the little girl was already there, talking excitedly about their afternoon's adventure. Octavia sat down, accepted sherry from Lucas and joined in the conversation in what she hoped was a perfectly normal manner so that, on the surface at least, the meal was a pleasant one. At least it was pleasant enough until Lucas said casually:

'Berendina, I'm taking Octavia to England for a few days tomorrow—Tante Lucilla wants you to go and stay with her while we're there—will you do that? I'll drive you over tomorrow—and don't argue, *lieveling*, if we're all away it gives Mrs Stubbs a few days of spoiling from the others—they're all longing to look after her, but with us around there isn't the time.'

Berendina instantly agreed with this. 'Though I'd like you to take me with you, Papa.'

'Not this time, love, but I promise you that we'll go to England at Christmas and you shall be taken to a pantomime there.'

Berendina whooped with delight. 'Octavia—Octavia, did you hear Papa? We're all going to the pantomime—I went last year and it was *fantastis!*'

Octavia had heard all right. She was looking across the table at Lucas, her pretty mouth open, the picture of amazement. 'Tomorrow? But that's so soon…'

'You'll have the whole day in which to do whatever has to be done,' he pointed out suavely, 'and Juffrouw Hinksma can cope with everything while we're away.'

Octavia had another try. 'Couldn't Berendina…' she began, and was brought to a halt by his quick 'No'. He sounded angry, although his promise to take Berendina to her aunt's house directly after lunch the next day was uttered in the most good-humoured of voices.

They left in the early evening in an atmosphere of cool friendliness which Octavia found daunting. Lucas had taken Berendina up to Groningen in the early afternoon, returned home just before six o'clock, accepted a cup of coffee, had a few words with Daan while Charlie put their cases in the boot, and then set out again. They would dine on the way, he explained to Octavia, as he had to call at a hospital in Rotterdam—a brief visit only.

He glanced at her, sitting quietly beside him in the corduroy suit, the new raincoat on the back seat. It was getting chilly now, but she had had no time to buy herself a winter coat, though she didn't think he would notice that. She was quite wrong. When they reached Rotterdam and stopped in the forecourt of the Anzia Ziekenhuis Lucas got out, took a large box from the boot and put it on the seat beside her.

'You've had no opportunity to get yourself a thick coat,' he observed. 'You may need this on the journey.' He didn't wait for her to speak but turned on his heel and went into the hospital.

Octavia eyed the expensive-looking box beside her and wondered if this was his way of apologising, or was he merely making sure that his wife was adequately dressed? She should of course have thought about buying a coat for the winter; she had more than enough money. Perhaps he thought she didn't dress well enough. She untied the thick cords and lifted the lid. There was a cashmere coat inside; rich brown, thick and soft. She drew it out carefully, opened the door, stepped into the forecourt and tried it on. It was a splendid fit as far as she could see and once it was on, she couldn't bear to take it off again. She got back into the Rolls, still wearing it, and when she went to replace the lid she saw that she had overlooked a little fur cap which matched the coat exactly. She tried that on too and was still admiring it in the car mirror when Lucas came back.

She waited until he was beside her. 'Lucas, I can never thank you enough! It's beautiful—I've never had anything so gorgeous in my life before. You're—you're too good to me, and I've been such a disappointment to you…'

'Did I say that?' He had turned to look at her with a faintly amused air.

'No, but I know I have—about yesterday, I mean. I don't quite know why you've given me this—you were so angry—I think you still are.' And as he remained silent: 'I should have bought a coat—is that why? You expect your wife to be well dressed and I…'

His voice was quiet. 'Shall we say no more about it? And yes, I do like to see my wife well dressed.'

He started the car and slid into the mass of traffic outside the hospital, and Octavia stared unseeingly out of her window; really there was nothing to say, just as he had said.

They stopped in Vlaardingen to dine at the Delta restaurant, and Octavia would have enjoyed it enormously if only she had felt happier. The combination of a wonderful coat, luxury restaurant and delicious food was quite heady. As it was she carried on a painfully polite conversation with Lucas uttering platitudes while her head was a wild muddle of questions she didn't dare ask.

It was only the next morning as they drove through the quiet early morning countryside that she found the courage to ask: 'Have you decided what to do with the house?'

He turned to look at her with faintly raised brows. 'My dear, it is your home—your former home. I'm bringing you back so that you may decide what you want to do about it.'

'Oh—I thought…' she stopped. 'It was so sudden—us coming, I mean. I expect you'd like me to sell it?'

'Not unless you want to. I had thought that you might like to keep it as a pleasant retreat.'

'I'd like that very much—Berendina would like it too.' A girl of persistence, she reiterated: 'Why did we come so suddenly? Did you have a reason?'

'I did.' He sounded curt. 'Would you like to stay in London for a night or go straight to Alresford?'

Octavia allowed her thoughts to dwell longingly on that and then dismissed them briskly. 'I think I'd like to go straight there, thank you.'

Her old home looked just the same. There was no sign of neglect; the brass door knocker shone as though it had just been polished, the windows sparkled and as they reached the door Mrs Lovelace opened it.

'There you are, my dears,' she said comfortably, just as though they had only been away for an hour or so. 'You'll find everything just as you wanted, sir, and it's a treat to see Miss Octavia again—such a lovely coat too!'

She beamed at them both as she stood aside to let them into the hall, accepted Octavia's delighted hug with pleasure and took the hand Lucas held out. 'I hope you'll find everything just so, sir,' she repeated.

No doubt of that, thought Octavia, sniffing fresh flowers, furniture polish and a delicious aroma from the kitchen. She glanced enquiringly at Lucas as he helped her off with her coat. 'It seemed a good idea,' he observed mildly, 'and Mrs Lovelace has been so kind as to agree to come in regularly.' He looked at that lady and smiled. 'You can manage to come in each day while we're here, Mrs Lovelace? Three days from eight in the morning until after lunch?'

Mrs Lovelace gave a comfortable chuckle. 'Well, of course, sir, and don't you worry, I'll keep the place nice and keep an eye on that gardener for you.'

'Gardener?' questioned Octavia.

'You have such a charming garden,' said Lucas at his most urbane. 'I took the opportunity of engaging a man to come in regularly and keep it in order.'

She looked away so that he wouldn't see the tears in her eyes and then thanked him in a trembly voice which he ignored. 'I've made an appointment with Mr Pimm for this afternoon, if you're agreeable?' They had gone into the sitting room, nice and warm because Mrs Lovelace had switched on the electric fire much earlier. 'Just a few papers for you to sign—giving him authority to pay wages and rates, and so on. There will be an account in your name at the bank…'

'Oh—did Father leave some money after all?'

Lucas didn't answer at once. Octavia listened to Mrs Lovelace in the kitchen, rattling plates and cutlery, until he said slowly: 'No—none at all, I'm afraid. Mr Pimm will explain.'

'Yes, but how can I pay wages if there isn't any money?'

'I have arranged for a sum of money to be deposited in your account at the bank here—sufficient to cover any expenses. And don't look like that, Octavia—it's a trifling sum.' His firm mouth twitched. 'I am well able to afford it.'

She turned round to look at him. 'Lucas, are you very rich? Marcus said you had a good deal more money than he had, and he doesn't work…'

'Yes, I am very rich, but he has more than enough to live on. He can support a wife and children with the greatest of ease, should he wish to do so.'

'Oh, that's good, because he intends to marry.' She smiled at the memory of Marcus's earnest face and Lucas, watching her, winced. But all he said was: 'Shall we have lunch? Mrs Lovelace is banging plates around in the dining room.'

Two days went by, largely filled by visits to Mr Pimm, who talked a good deal in dry-as-dust terms about money and property tax and rates of interest. Octavia, confident that Lucas was taking it all in and would explain it to her later if necessary, allowed her thoughts to wander. Her home would be a lovely place to visit—just now and then, with Berendina, of course, and Lucas… She allowed her thoughts to become daydreams, then, filling her head with delightful pictures of them both with Berendina and at least two small replicas of Lucas, spending a week or so in the little house with Mrs Lovelace to do the work while they spent their days picnicking. There were only four bedrooms, of course; supposing they had a really large family? Bunk beds in the biggest guest room, or would the boys be tough enough to camp in the garden? She was debating this tricky point when Lucas's voice brought her back to the everyday world.

She hadn't heard what he had said, but he obviously wanted her to sign something or other. She did so without bothering to read it and went back to her daydreaming.

And later, when she thanked him for all the trouble he was taking, he had very little to say, only pointing out quietly: 'Should you wish to stay here at any time, it will be easy enough for you to do so. There is money enough in your account to keep you going for some time.'

She eyed him in some doubt. 'Lucas, what do you mean? Why should I want to come here by myself? I…' She stopped, struck by the horrid thought that if he were regretting their marriage and wanted to bring it to a dignified conclusion, all the arrangements which had been made would be a convenient means to an end. She said in a subdued voice: 'I do thank you, Lucas,' and then rather defiantly: 'Perhaps I shall do just that.'

He didn't reply, and muttering something about getting the supper Octavia took herself off to the kitchen where her strong feelings caused her to over-salt the vegetables, serve the meat horribly underdone, and burn the custard. Lucas ate his way through these horrors without comment, but over the cup of instant coffee she offered him he suggested equably that they might leave on the following day, since their business with the house was done, and spend a night in London. 'We must find something for Berendina,' he observed, 'and you may want to do some shopping—we might go to a theatre.'

Octavia agreed at once. Never mind what the future held, a stay in London with Lucas wasn't to be missed. She went to the kitchen to fetch a tray and he, having poured his coffee into the nearest pot plant, sat back in his chair with his eyes closed, a faint frown on his face.

They left after breakfast in a wintry sunshine and a piercing wind which made Octavia thankful for her sables, stopping for coffee on the way and reaching London well before lunch time. They had talked in a desultory fashion about nothing in particular, but now, as Lucas slowed the Rolls and began making his way through Kensington, Octavia asked: 'Where are we to stay?'

'The Connaught.' He was driving smoothly through Knightsbridge now and presently turned into Mount Street and stopped before the doors of the hotel. Octavia took a quick look and was thankful for the sables; it was that kind of an hotel. A faintly anxious look crept over her pretty face and Lucas understood it. 'We might go shopping after lunch,' he suggested. 'You'll need a dress, I expect.'

She had a magnificent room, but she felt lost in its splendid comfort. She found herself longing for the house in den Haag and hurried a little over the tidying of her person so that she was quite ready when Lucas came for her. Over lunch he asked her if she would like to go to a theatre that evening and when she said that she would prefer to remain in the hotel and dance after dinner, looked surprised.

She saw the look and said at once: 'Oh, have you already got tickets? Or would you rather not dance? I don't mind; I shall love whatever we do.'

He assured her that he would enjoy dancing too before suggesting that if she had finished her lunch it might be a good idea if she were to fetch her coat so that they might go shopping.

They took a taxi to Fortnum and Mason, where Lucas

maintained they would find something for Berendina. And they did, a white fur hat and muff, at a price which staggered Octavia although, Berendina being Berendina, she was worth every penny of it, and when Lucas accompanied her to the gown department she was staggered again, but since he remained remarkably calm at even the most extravagant prices, she allowed herself to be persuaded into buying a rose-patterned organza dress with full sleeves caught into lace-edged frills at the elbows, a wide, wide skirt and a neckline which rather shocked her. But there again Lucas observed in his most moderate tones that it became her very well, so she supposed that if he liked it, she did too. She bought slippers too and an enchanting little handbag which happened to catch her eye.

They had tea in the tea-rooms there and then wandered along, looking in all the shop windows, buying a great box of chocolates for Berendina and tobacco for Charlie and Daan, as well as scarves and handkerchiefs for everyone else. They walked back to the hotel, burdened with parcels, and presently dined, Octavia in the new dress, her head crowded with a mixture of sheer happiness because she was with Lucas and misery because he was behaving towards her as though she were a friend of the family who had to be entertained at all costs. Because of that she hardly noticed the delicious food put before her, although she drank a little too much of the champagne he ordered, so that later, when they danced, she felt a little dizzy, and the champagne having drowned the misery for the moment, she danced like a fairy in his arms, not speaking, but smiling up at him, her slightly befuddled mind not registering his austere expression.

It was only hours later, when she was in bed and the effects of the champagne had worn off, that she remembered that and wondered uneasily if she had said or done anything to annoy him. Indeed, at breakfast after a poor night, she asked him. 'Because I think I had a little too much champagne last night,' she confessed. 'Did—did I say anything?'

He surveyed her over his coffee cup, his eyes twinkling. 'No, Octavia, nothing.'

'Oh, good!'

The twinkle had gone, and he said gravely: 'Was there something you were afraid you might have said?'

She could only be honest with him; when one loved someone as much as she loved him, one couldn't be anything else. 'Well, yes, but as long as I didn't say it, it doesn't matter.'

She thought he was angry, although he said mildly enough: 'Then that settles the matter. What would you like to do this morning? Shopping again or a walk in the park?'

Octavia chose the walk and fed the ducks with the rolls Lucas had obligingly bought for her and after lunch, at his suggestion, they strolled along to the Burlington Arcade, where, again at his suggestion, she bought a silk scarf, several pairs of gloves and a mohair sweater for Berendina and then, because they were so soft and pretty, one for herself. It disappointed her considerably when Lucas, rather curtly, refused her offer to buy him one too. Perhaps, she consoled herself, he was a man who liked to buy his own clothes.

They travelled back that evening, an uneventful journey, and it seemed to her that the nearer they got to den Haag, the more abstracted Lucas became, although once they were home, with Berendina, allowed to miss school for the morning, dancing round them and everyone there to welcome them back, she decided that she had been imagining it, for he was his usual pleasant self, handing out packages and answering his small daughter's flow of excited questions. But he didn't stay long; there were cases at the hospital, he explained, and he would probably be back late.

And during the next week Octavia hardly saw him at all; and on the only day when he came home early, Marcus was on the telephone, telling her that he had persuaded Iona to marry him at last, although he still had to find a job. She had looked up as Lucas came in and smiled. 'Hullo, how nice—you're home early. I'll ask for tea,' and then to Marcus: 'I'm going to ring off, Marcus, Lucas has just come in.'

Lucas had been going towards the small sitting room. Now he turned sharply and opened his study door. 'No tea, thank you,' he said quietly, 'I've some work to do.'

Octavia eyed him anxiously at dinner later that evening, on the point of asking him if he felt all right; he had been working too hard and too long and she would have said so, only he rendered her dumb with his silky denial of anything amiss and went on to ask her if the following Saturday suited her to invite the Burgermeester and his lady to dinner. She agreed at once, her head full of the fearful idea that perhaps he had fallen in love with someone else. She surprised herself as well as him when she asked suddenly: 'Do you ever think about Margriet?'

He raised his eyebrows. 'Should I?'

She said impatiently: 'How should I know?' She twiddled her wine glass between her fingers, staring at it. 'Do you still love her?'

He took so long to answer that she added: 'I really want to know, Lucas.'

'No, Octavia, I don't love her—I remember her with some sort of affection, I suppose, but I had ceased to love her soon after our marriage.' He added, a nasty edge to his voice: 'Have you any more questions?'

She put the glass down carefully. 'No—no, thank you for telling me.'

He had gone out again directly afterwards.

Saturday was still three days away. Octavia went to her Dutch lessons, took Berendina to school and fetched her home, did the flowers, conferred with some difficulty with Juffrouw Hinksma about the menu for their august guests, and took Mrs Stubbs, still not quite herself, for one or two short runs through the countryside. But although she kept herself busy, she knew that without a doubt, she was going to tell Lucas that she would have to go away, that she loved him and that living in his house, never seeing him and when she did, behaving as though he were a stranger, was an impossibility.

Dressing on Saturday evening, she decided to speak to him that very evening. He had been out with Berendina all the morning and in the afternoon had shut himself up in his study. She had waited for him to come out, but when he did it was to answer a call at the hospital.

She was dressed and hanging about in the hall when he returned. He looked tired, she thought, and withdrawn, but she was too anxious to have her say to care about that. She hurried to meet him, her lovely dress—the one she had bought at Fortnum and Mason—floating around her, the family diamonds winking and sparkling in the light of the great chandelier.

'Lucas, there you are! I must talk to you…'

He had thrown his overcoat on to a chair, and was on his way to his study with his briefcase. Now he paused to say: 'Not now, Octavia—the Burgermeester and his lady are punctual people.'

'Blow the Burgermeester, and his lady!' snapped

Octavia crossly. 'There's something I must tell you—I should have told you days ago, but I—I didn't have the nerve.'

Lucas stood very still, his face white. 'And this—whatever it is which is so important—whom does it concern?'

She was so pleased that he was going to listen that she blurted out: 'Marcus—and me, of course.'

He said in a very level voice: 'Of course.' He glanced at his watch. 'I'll be down in twenty minutes, that should give us time in which to talk. You won't wait until our guests have gone?'

'No,' said Octavia very positively. 'I've screwed up my courage and I won't be put off.'

He didn't say anything to this but turned on his heel and started up the staircase. She watched his broad back and felt desolate.

He was as good as his word, coming quietly to join her in the drawing room, elegant in his dinner jacket, calm and self-assured, but still, she saw unhappily, bone-weary, so that she asked: 'Would you like a drink?'

'No—you had something to tell me, and since you insist upon telling me now, had you not better begin?' And when she stayed silent: 'You said that it was about you and Marcus. I am not altogether surprised, you know; he is your age, amusing and with time on his hands.'

Octavia had never heard his voice so bitter.

She broke in eagerly: 'Yes, but Lucas, he's going to get a job—you see, Iona Hendriks won't marry him unless he does. That's why he was telephoning me the other day.'

She was looking away from him as she spoke, so that she missed the expression on his face, and when he said urgently: 'Octavia, you must…' she cried: 'No, don't try and stop me—I haven't finished. It's about me now. I can't stay here, really I can't—you see, I love you so, Lucas. I thought just for a little while…' she paused and gulped like a child trying not to cry. 'But when we went to Alresford last week I guessed that you were making plans—I mean, for me to go back there to live…'

She was interrupted by his thundering roar. 'My dear, dear darling!' He had crossed the room in a couple of enormous strides and clasped her so tightly that she could hardly breathe, careless of the gossamer of her dress. 'I love you, I think I always have, although I didn't know it until that night when we did that ectopic. I made up my mind to marry you then. You liked me, I knew that, and I was sure that I could make you love me in time. Only when I saw you with Marcus I was filled with doubts…' He bent and kissed her with slow enjoyment. 'I kept away as much as I could. It was hell, but I thought that if you fell in love with Marcus and wanted to leave me it would be easier for you if you had the house at Alresford to go to.'

Octavia stared up at him. 'I don't care tuppence for Marcus. I never did—I know he's your cousin, but he's an idle boy.' She flung her arms round his neck and reached up to kiss him fiercely. 'I want to be your wife and know about your work and be here when you come home each day and choose your ties… Lucas, oh, Lucas!' She smiled a wide, rather quivering smile. 'And Berendina wants a nursery full of babies to boss around.'

For which satisfactory speech she was soundly kissed once more and so thoroughly that she didn't at once hear the rich vibrations of the door bell. When they at length penetrated her senses, she broke away for an inch or two to exclaim: 'Lucas, the Burgermeester!' And then: 'Lucas, do you really love me?'

'Yes, my darling, and never while the grass grows shall I cease to love you.'

He clamped her close again and fell to kissing her again, so that she resigned herself happily to forgetting about their guests, dinner, and everything else in the world except their two selves. Only when voices were heard in the hall did Lucas stop kissing her, and then reluctantly, to twitch her round; eyes sparkling, hair delightfully ruffled, cheeks pink, to stand beside him and face the door which Daan was opening to admit the Burgermeester and his lady.

* * * * *

New York Times and *USA TODAY* bestselling author *Maya Banks* presents a brand-new miniseries

PREGNANCY & PASSION

When four irresistible tycoons face the consequences of temptation.

Book 1—ENTICED BY HIS FORGOTTEN LOVER

Available September 2011 from Harlequin® Desire®!

Rafael de Luca had been in bad situations before. A crowded ballroom could never make him sweat.

These people would never know that he had no memory of any of them.

He surveyed the party with grim tolerance, searching for the source of his unease.

At first his gaze flickered past her, but he yanked his attention back to a woman across the room. Her stare bored holes through him. Unflinching and steady, even when his eyes locked with hers.

Petite, even in heels, she had a creamy olive complexion. A wealth of inky-black curls cascaded over her shoulders and her eyes were equally dark.

She looked at him as if she'd already judged him and found him lacking. He'd never seen her before in his life. Or had he?

He cursed the gaping hole in his memory. He'd been diagnosed with selective amnesia after his accident four months ago. Which seemed like complete and utter bull. No one got amnesia except hysterical women in bad soap operas.

With a smile, he disengaged himself from the group

HDEXP0911

around him and made his way to the mystery woman.

She wasn't coy. She stared straight at him as he approached, her chin thrust upward in defiance.

"Excuse me, but have we met?" he asked in his smoothest voice.

His gaze moved over the generous swell of her breasts pushed up by the empire waist of her black cocktail dress.

When he glanced back up at her face, he saw fury in her eyes.

"Have we *met?*" Her voice was barely a whisper, but he felt each word like the crack of a whip.

Before he could process her response, she nailed him with a right hook. He stumbled back, holding his nose.

One of his guards stepped between Rafe and the woman, accidentally sending her to one knee. Her hand flew to the folds of her dress.

It was then, as she cupped her belly, that the realization hit him. She was pregnant.

Her eyes flashing, she turned and ran down the marble hallway.

Rafael ran after her. He burst from the hotel lobby, and saw two shoes sparkling in the moonlight, twinkling at him.

He blew out his breath in frustration and then shoved the pair of sparkly, ultrafeminine heels at his head of security.

"Find the woman who wore these shoes."

HDEXP0911